汉英对照阅读系列
Chinese-English Readers series

Straw Houses
草房子

Better Link Press

目

录

CONTENTS

致读者

要学好一种语言，必须多听、多说、多读、多写。要学好汉语也不例外，必须多听普通话，多阅读汉语作品。

《文化中国·汉英对照阅读丛书》是一套开放的系列，收入其中的主要为当代中国作家的散文、故事、小说等。我们编辑这套汉英对照读物的目的是帮助你阅读欣赏原汁原味的当代中国文学或非文学作品，让你在学习现代汉语、提高汉语阅读水平的同时，了解中国社会、中国文化、中国历史，以及当代中国人民的生活。我们采用汉英对照的办法，是为了帮助你更好地欣赏这些作品，对照英语译文你可以知道自己是不是真正正确地理解了这些汉语原作的意思。

希望你能喜欢。

—— 编者

To the Reader

Acquisition of proficiency in a foreign language calls for diligent practices in listening, speaking, reading, and writing. Learning Chinese is no exception. To a student of Chinese, extensive reading exercises are as important as constant exposure to spoken Mandarin.

Cultural China: Chinese-English Readers series is an open-ended series of collections of writings in Chinese, mostly essays and short stories by contemporary Chinese writers. Our purpose in putting together this bilingual series is to help you enjoy contemporary Chinese literature and other writings in their authentic, unadulterated flavor and to understand the Chinese society, culture, history, and the contemporary life of the Chinese people as you learn the language and hone your reading skills. A bilingual text will assist you in better savoring these works and in checking your understanding of the Chinese original against the English translation.

We hope you will like this volume.

– the Editor

关于《草房子》和曹文轩

《草房子》是一部围绕小男孩桑桑的经历展开的儿童读物。小说从桑桑的视角讲述几个看似寻常而又极为感人的故事，展示了生活中令人感动的时刻和桑桑的内心世界。本书仅摘取了小说中的两章。

《草房子》以二十世纪六十年代早期的江南水乡为背景，文字简洁明快。小说于1997年出版后，被誉为中国儿童文学史上的里程碑。

作者曹文轩，1954年1月出生于江苏省，现为北大中国文学教授，中国作家协会会员，北京作协副主席。他的作品以风格纯美著称，曾两次获宋庆龄儿童文学奖并获安徒生奖提名。主要作品有《草房子》、《红瓦》、《根鸟》、《红葫芦》和《三角地》。

About *Straw Houses* and Cao Wenxuan

Straw Houses is a children's book that details the little boy Sang Sang's experience. It includes several seemingly ordinary yet touching stories, all told and presented through Sang Sang's point of view, revealing not only the touching moments of human life but also Sang Sang's inner psychology. Here in this book are only two chapters from the original novel.

Set in the early 1960s in the area south of the Yangtze River in China, *Straw Houses* is told in a language that highlights simplicity and serenity. The novel, first published in 1997, has been called a landmark in the history of Chinese children's literature.

Born in Jan 1954 in Jiangsu Province, Cao Wenxuan is a professor of Chinese literature at Beijing University, member of the National Committee of Writers' Association of Beijing. Professor Cao, famous for the aesthetic inclination of his works, is a two-time top prize winner of Soong Ching Ling Children's Literature Award, and he was nominated for the Hans Christian Andersen Awards. His literary works include *Straw Houses, The Red Tiles, Gen Niao, The Red Gourd* and *Sanjiaodi.*

那是1962年8月的一个上午，秋风乍起，暑气已去，十四岁的男孩桑桑，登上了油麻地小学那一片草房子中间最高一幢的房顶。他坐在屋脊上，油麻地小学第一次一下子就全都扑进了他的眼底。秋天的白云，温柔如絮，悠悠远去；梧桐的枯叶，正在秋风里忽闪忽闪地飘落。这个男孩桑桑，忽然觉得自己想哭，于是就小声地呜咽起来。

明天一大早，一只大木船，在油麻地还未醒来时，就将载着他和他的家，远远地离开这里——他将永远地告别与他朝夕相伴的这片金色的草房子。

One morning in August 1962, the autumn wind had begun its assault and the summer heat had retreated. Sang Sang, a 14 year-old boy, climbed onto the rooftop of the highest building in a stretch of straw houses at the Youmadi Primary School. He sat on the ridge, immediately taking the whole of Youmadi Primary School in his view for the very first time. The white clouds of autumn were as soft as cotton wadding, drifting away in leisure. The withered leaves of Chinese parasol fell down in the autumn wind intermittently, glittering. The boy Sang Sang suddenly wanted to cry and he sobbed in a low voice.

Very early the next morning, a big wooden boat would take him and his family far away, before Youmadi awoke. He would bid farewell to the stretch of golden straw houses which had kept him company day and night, and be gone for good.

纸月

1

纸月的外婆用手拉着纸月，出现在桑桑家的院子里时，是那年秋天的一个下午。那时，桑桑正在喂他的那群纯一色的白鸽。白鸽受了陌生人的惊扰，呼啦一声飞了起来。这时，桑桑一眼看到了纸月：她被白鸽的突然起飞与那么强烈的翅响惊得紧紧搂住外婆的胳膊，靠在外婆的身上，微微缩着脖子，还半眯着眼睛，生怕鸽子的翅膀会打着她似的。

白鸽在天上盘旋着。当时正有着秋天最好的阳光，鸽群从天空滑过时，天空中闪着迷人的白光。这些小家伙，居然在见了陌生人之后，产生了表演的欲望，在空中潇洒而优美地展翅、滑翔或作集体性的俯冲、拔高与穿梭。

桑桑看到了外婆身旁一张微仰着的脸、一对乌黑乌黑的眼睛。

白鸽们终于像倒转的旋风，朝下盘旋，然后又纷纷落进院子里，发出一片咕咕声。

纸月慢慢地从受了惊吓的状态里出来，渐渐松开外婆的胳膊，好奇而又欢喜地看着这一地雪团样的白鸽。

Zhi Yue

I

On one autumn afternoon, Zhi Yue's grandmother held her hand and appeared in Sang Sang's courtyard. Sang Sang was feeding a flock of white pigeons. Startled, the white pigeons flapped their wings hard and flew away. Sang Sang immediately saw Zhi Yue, who was startled by the abruptness of the pigeons' movements and the heavy sound of their flapping wings. She held her grandmother's arm tightly and leaned on her body. She tucked in her head slightly and closed her eyes halfway, as if she were afraid the pigeons' wings would strike her.

The white pigeons circled above. It was an autumn day, splendid with sunshine. As the flock of pigeons flew across, they glistened beautifully in the sky. Having seen an audience, they were tempted to perform, stretching their wings and gliding freely and beautifully in the sky, or diving and flying up and across.

Sang Sang saw a face looking slightly upward, a pair of black eyes beside her grandmother.

Finally, white pigeons descended to the courtyard like a falling whirlwind, making cooing noises as they landed.

Zhi Yue recovered and loosened her grip on her grandmother's arm. She looked at the snow-white pigeons in surprise and joy.

“这里是桑校长家吗?”纸月的外婆问。

桑桑点点头。

“你是桑桑?”纸月的外婆拉着纸月往前走了一步。

桑桑点点头，但用疑惑的目光望着纸月的外婆：你是怎么知道我叫桑桑的?

“谁都知道，桑校长家有个长得很俊的男孩，叫桑桑。”

桑桑突然不安起来，因为，他看到了自己的样子：没有穿鞋，两只光脚脏兮兮的；裤子被胯骨勉强地挂住，一只裤管耷拉在脚面，而另一只裤管却卷到了膝盖以上；褂子因与人打架，缺了两颗纽扣，而两只小口袋，也被人撕得只有一点点连着。

“你爸爸在家吗?”纸月的外婆问。

“在。”桑桑趁机跑进屋里，“爸，有人找。”

桑乔走了出来。他认识纸月的外婆，便招呼纸月的外婆与纸月进屋。

纸月还是拉着外婆的手，一边望着鸽子，一边轻手轻脚地走着，生怕再惊动了它们。而鸽子并不怕纸月，其中一只，竟然跑到了纸月的脚下来啄一粒玉米。纸月就赶紧停住不走，直到外婆用力拉了她一下，才侧着身子走过去。

桑桑没有进屋，但桑桑很注意地听着屋子里的对话——

“这丫头叫纸月。”

"Is this principal Sang's home?" Zhi Yue's grandmother asked.

Sang Sang nodded.

"Are you Sang Sang?" Zhi Yue's grandmother moved a step forward, tugging Zhi Yue with her.

Sang Sang nodded. He gave Zhi Yue's grandmother a puzzled look. "How did you know I was Sang Sang?"

"Everyone knows there is a good-looking boy called Sang Sang at principal Sang's home."

Sang Sang suddenly felt embarrassed. He realized how he looked: no shoes, dirty bare feet; his hipbone just managed to support his trousers; one trouser leg drooped over his foot, the other was rolled above his knee. He had had a fight, and two buttons were missing on his coat. The two little pockets were torn and only managed to hang on.

"Is your father in?" Zhi Yue's grandmother asked.

"Yes." Sang Sang took the opportunity to run into the house. "Father, there is someone here looking for you."

Sang Qiao walked out. He knew Zhi Yue's grandmother. He greeted them and invited them in.

Zhi Yue still held her grandmother's hand. She watched the pigeons, moving lightly so as not to startle them again. But now the pigeons didn't fear Zhi Yue; one of them even came to Zhi Yue's feet to peck at an ear of maize. Zhi Yue stopped until her grandmother tugged her hard. She turned and walked in.

Sang Sang didn't enter the room, but he listened to the conversation attentively from outside.

"She is called Zhi Yue."

“这名字好听。”

“我想把纸月转到您的学校来上学。”

“那为什么呢？”

停顿了一阵，纸月的外婆说：“也不为什么。只是纸月这孩子不想再在板仓小学念书了。”

“这恐怕不行呀。上头有规定，小孩就地上学。纸月就该在板仓小学上学。再说，孩子来这儿上学也很不方便，从板仓走到油麻地，要走三里路。”

“她能走。”

屋里没有声音了。过了一会儿，父亲说：“您给我出难题了。”

“让她来吧。孩子不想在那儿念书了。”

“纸月，”父亲的声音，“这么远的路，你走得动吗？”

停了停，纸月说：“我走得动。”

过了一会儿，父亲说：“我们再商量商量吧。”

“我和纸月谢谢您了。”

桑桑紧接着听到了父亲吃惊的声音：“大妈，别这样别这样！”桑桑走到门口往屋里看了一眼，只见外婆拉着纸月正要在父亲面前跪下来，被父亲一把扶住了。

随即，桑桑听到了外婆与纸月的轻轻的啜泣声。

桑桑蹲在地上，呆呆地看着他的鸽子。

父亲说：“再过两天就开学了，您就让孩子来吧。”

纸月和外婆走出屋子，来到院子里，正要往外走时，桑

" A nice name."

"I want to transfer her to your school."

"Why?"

After a pause, Zhi Yue's grandmother said, "Nothing special. It's just that Zhi Yue doesn't want to go to Bancang Primary School anymore."

"This is difficult. It is a rule that children go to nearest school. Zhi Yue should go to Bancang Primary School. What's more, it is inconvenient for her to come here -- she would have to walk three li."

"She can walk."

There was no sound. After a while, Sang Sang's father said, "It is really difficult."

"Let her come. She doesn't want to study there."

"Zhi Yue," Sang Sang's father said, "Can you really walk such a distance?"

A pause, then Zhi Yue said, "Yes I can."

After a while, the father said, "We will have to look into it."

"Zhi Yue and I thank you."

Sang Sang heard his father's startled voice. "Oh, please, don't do this!" Sang Sang walked to the door and glanced inside. He saw that Zhi Yue's grandmother had pulled Zhi Yue and they were about to kneel down in front of his father. His father had stopped her.

Sang Sang heard the grandmother and Zhi Yue sobbing.

He squatted, in a trance, watching his pigeons.

His father said, "The term starts in two days' time. OK, let Zhi Yue come."

Zhi Yue and her grandmother walked outside the room to

桑的母亲挎着竹篮从菜园里回来了。桑桑的母亲一见了纸月，就喜欢上了："这小丫头，真体面。"

几个大人，又说起了纸月转学的事。母亲说："遇到刮风下雨天，纸月就在我家吃饭，就在我家住。"母亲望着纸月，目光里满是怜爱。当母亲忽然注意到桑桑时，说："桑桑，你看看人家纸月，浑身上下这么干干净净的，你看你那双手，剁下来狗都不闻。"

桑桑和纸月都把手藏到了身后。桑桑藏住的是一双满是污垢的黑乎乎的手，纸月藏住的却是一双白净的细嫩如笋的手。

纸月和她的外婆走后，桑桑的父亲与母亲就一直在说纸月家的事。桑桑就在一旁听着，将父亲与母亲支离破碎的话连成了一个完整的故事：

纸月的母亲是这一带长得最水灵的女子。后来，她怀孕了，肚皮一日一日地隆起来。但谁也不知道这孩子是谁的，她也不说，只是一声不吭地让孩子在她的肚子里一天一天地大起来。纸月的外婆似乎也没有太多地责备纸月的母亲，只是做她应该做的事情。纸月的母亲在怀着纸月的时候，依然是那么的好看，只是脸色一天比一天苍白，眼窝一天比一天深陷下去。她不常出门，大多数时间就是在屋子里给将要出生的纸月做衣服做鞋。她在那些衣服与裤子上绣上了她最喜欢的花，一针一线的，都很认真。秋天，当田野间的野菊花开出一片黄的与淡紫的小花朵时，纸月出世了。一个月后，纸月的母亲在一天的黄昏离开了家门。两天后，人们在四周长满菖蒲的水塘里找到

the courtyard. Just then, Sang Sang's mother came back from the vegetable garden with a bamboo basket. She saw Zhi Yue and immediately liked her. "Such a nice girl."

The adults talked about Zhi Yue. Sang Sang's mother said, "When it is windy or raining, Zhi Yue can come to have meals and stay with us." The mother looked at Zhi Yue affectionately. She suddenly noticed Sang Sang and said, "Look at Zhi Yue. She is so clean. And look at your hands. If I chop them off, even the dog wouldn't touch them."

Sang Sang and Zhi Yue both hid their hands behind them. He hid a pair of grimy, stained hands while hers were white, clean, delicate and as tender as bamboo shoots.

When Zhi Yue and her grandmother had gone, Sang Sang's parents discussed Zhi Yue's family. Sang Sang listened, and managed to put the pieces into a complete story.

Zhi Yue's mother was the prettiest young woman in the neighborhood. She was pregnant and her belly was swelling by the day. Nobody knew who the father was, though, and she didn't say. She kept her silence and allowed her child to grow in her belly. Zhi Yue's grandmother didn't blame her too much; she just did what she could do. Even though carrying a baby, Zhi Yue's mother was still very pretty. But she was getting paler and her eyes were sinking in their sockets. She didn't go out often. Most of her time was spent making clothes and shoes for the coming baby Zhi Yue. She sewed her favorite flowers on the clothes, thread by thread, very attentively. In autumn, when wild chrysanthemums were yielding yellow and pale purple flowers in the fields, Zhi Yue was born. One month later, at dusk, her mother left home, and another two days later, she

了她。从此，纸月的外婆，既作为纸月的外婆，又作为纸月的母亲，一日一日，默默地将小小的纸月抚养。

关于纸月为什么要从板仓小学转到油麻地小学来读书，桑桑的父亲的推测是："板仓小学那边肯定有坏孩子欺负纸月。"

桑桑的母亲听了，倚在门框上，长长地叹了一口气……

2

桑桑向母亲提出他要有一件新褂子，理由是马上就要开学了，他应该有一件新褂子。

母亲说："这是太阳从西边出来了，你也知道要新衣服了。"就很快去镇上扯回布来，领着桑桑去一个做缝纫活的人家量了身长，并让人家尽快将活做出来。

开学头一天下午，桑桑跑到水码头，将衣服脱了扔在草上，然后撩着河水洗着身子。秋后的河水已经很凉了。桑桑一激灵一激灵的，在水码头上不停地跳，又颤颤抖抖地把那些乡谣大声叫唤出来：

姐姐十五我十六，
妈生姐姐我煮粥。
爸爸睡在摇篮里，
没有奶吃向我哭。
记得外公娶外婆，

was found in a pond full of cattails. Zhi Yue's grandmother assumed the role of mother and quietly brought Zhi Yue up.

Sang Sang's father guessed the reason why Zhi Yue wanted to transfer from Bancang to Youmadi: "There must be bad kids bullying Zhi Yue there."

Sang Sang's mother leaned on the door frame and sighed deeply...

2

Sang Sang asked his mother for new clothes. Soon, the new term would begin, so he should have new clothes.

His mother said, "Is the sun coming up from the west? You want new clothes?!" But she was quick to get some cloth from town. Then she took Sang Sang to a tailor for measurements and asked the tailor to quickly make new clothes.

The afternoon before the new term, Sang Sang went to the quay, took his old clothes off and threw them on the grass. He washed himself in the river. It was late autumn and the water was already quite chilly. Sang Sang felt fists of cold. He jumped repeatedly on the quay, and shakily sang country ballads :

Sister is 15 and I'm 16,
Mum gave birth to sister, but I was cooking congee.
Papa slept in the cradle,
He cried because there was no milk.
When grandpa married grandma,

我在轿前放爆竹。

就有人发笑，并将桑桑的母亲从屋里叫出来："看你家桑桑在干什么呢。"

桑桑的母亲走到河边上，不知是因为桑桑的样子很好笑，还是因为桑桑大声嚷嚷着的乡谣很好笑，就绷不住脸笑了："小猴子，冻死你！"

桑桑转身对着母亲，用肥皂将自己擦得浑身是沫，依然不住声地大叫着。

桑桑的母亲过来要拉桑桑，桑桑就趁机往后一仰，跌进河里。

桑桑觉得自己总算洗得很干净了，才爬上岸。现在，桑桑的母亲见到的桑桑，是一个浑身被清冽的河水洗得通红、没有一星污垢的桑桑。

桑桑穿好衣服，说："我要去取我的白褂子。"说着就走了。

桑桑的衣服被搁下了，还没有做好。桑桑就坐在人家门槛上等。人家只好先把手里的活停下来做他的白褂子。桑桑直到把白褂子等到手才回家，那时天都黑了，村里人家都已亮灯了。回到家，桑桑的脑袋被正在吃饭的母亲用筷子敲了一下："这孩子，像等不及了。"

第二天，桑桑上学路过办公室门口时，首先是正在往池塘边倒药渣的温幼菊发现了桑桑。她惊讶地说："哎哟，桑桑，你要干吗？"

那时，各班老师都正准备往自己的教室走，见了整日泥猴一样甚至常不洗脸的桑桑，今日居然打扮成这样，都围

I was lighting the firecrackers.

People laughed and called Sang Sang's mother out to watch. "Look at what your Sang Sang is doing!"

Sang Sang's mother walked to the riverside. Was it because Sang Sang looked funny, or his song was funny? She couldn't hold her laugh. "Little monkey, aren't you cold?"

Sang Sang turned to face his mother; bubbles of soap covered him. He was still shouting.

Sang Sang's mother came to grab him. He leaned backward and fell in the river.

Sang Sang decided he was clean, and climbed onto the bank. His mother saw a dustless boy washed red by the cool water.

Sang Sang put on his clothes and said, "I'm going to get my white clothes." Then he left.

Sang Sang's new clothes weren't ready. He sat on the threshold to wait. The tailor had to put down what he was doing and work on Sang Sang's white clothes. Sang Sang didn't go home until they were ready. It was already dark and people had turned on their lights. When he got home, his mother, who was eating, hit him with her chopsticks. "Couldn't you wait, child?"

The next day, when Sang Sang passed the teacher's office on his way to school, Wen Youju was the first to see him. She was pouring the remains of herbal medicine in the pond. She was surprised, "Ah, Sang Sang, what's up?"

Head teachers of different classes were all walking towards their classrooms. They saw Sang Sang dressed like this today, and surrounded him. Sang Sang had always been like a muddy

过来看。六年级的语文老师朱恒问："桑桑，是有相亲的要来吗？"

桑桑说："去你的。"他自己也感觉到，他的小白褂子实在太白了，赶紧往自己的教室走。

桑桑进教室，又遭到同学们一阵哄笑。不知是谁喊了一声"小白褂"，随即全体响应："小白褂！小白褂……"

眼见着桑桑要恼了，他们才停止叫唤。

上课前一刻钟，正当教室里乱得听不清人语时，蒋一轮领着纸月出现在门口。教室里顿时安静下来。大家都在打量纸月：纸月上身穿着袖口大大的紫红色褂子，下身穿着裤管微微短了一点的蓝布裤子，背着一只墨绿色的绣了一朵红莲花的书包，正怯生生地看着大家。

"她叫纸月，是你们的新同学。"蒋一轮说。

"纸月？她叫纸月。"孩子们互相咀嚼着这一名字。

从此，纸月就成了桑桑的同学，一直到六年级第二学期初纸月突然离开草房子为止。

纸月坐下后，看了一眼桑桑，那时桑桑正趴在窗台上看他的鸽群。

纸月到油麻地小学读书，引起了一些孩子的疑惑：她为什么要跑这么远来上学呢？但过了几天，大家也就不再去疑惑了，仿佛纸月本来就是他们的一个同学。而纸月呢，畏畏缩缩地生疏了几天之后，也与大家慢慢熟起来。她先是与女生们说了话，后又与男生们说了话，一切都正常起来。唯一有

monkey and didn't even wash his face. Chinese language teacher of grade six Zhu Heng asked, "Sang Sang, are you seeing someone today?"

Sang Sang said, "Heck, no." He realized his white coat was indeed too white. He hurried to his classroom.

His classmates all laughed when he walked in. Someone shouted "little white coat!". And it was echoed all around, "Little white coat, little white coat..."

Sang Sang was getting mad, so they stopped.

Fifteen minutes before class, when it was very noisy in the classroom, Jiang Yilun appeared at the door with Zhi Yue. The classroom immediately became quiet. Everyone was eyeing Zhi Yue. She wore a purple-red coat with big cuffs, and slightly short blue cotton trousers. She had a dark blue bag embroidered with a red lotus flower. She looked at everyone timidly.

"This is Zhi Yue, your new classmate," said Jiang Yilun.

"Zhi Yue? She is called Zhi Yue," children mumbled the name to each other.

Zhi Yue became Sang Sang's classmate, until the second term of grade six, when she suddenly left the straw houses.

Zhi Yue sat down and looked at Sang Sang. Sang Sang leaned on the windowsill, watching his flock of pigeons.

Zhi Yue's coming to Youmadi Primary School had puzzled many children. Why did she come such a long distance for school? A few days later, they forgot it, as if Zhi Yue had always been their classmate. Zhi Yue, after being timid for a few days, became friendly with the others. She spoke with girls first, then with boys too. Things were normal, except that she hadn't

点奇怪的是：她还没有与她第一个见到的桑桑说过话。而桑桑呢，也从没有要主动与她说话的意思。不过，这也没有什么。总之，纸月觉得在油麻地小学读书，挺愉快的，那张显得有点苍白的脸上，总是微微地泛着红润。

不久，大家还知道了这一点：纸月原来是一个很了不起的女孩子。她的毛笔字大概要算是油麻地小学的学生中间写得最好的一个了。蒋一轮老师恨不得给纸月的大字簿上的每一个字都画上红色的圆圈。桑乔的毛笔字，是油麻地小学的老师中间写得最好的一个。他翻看了蒋一轮拿过来的纸月的大字簿，说："这孩子的字写得很秀丽，不骄不躁，是有来头的。"就让蒋一轮将纸月叫来，问她："你的字是谁教的？"纸月说："没有人教。"纸月走后，桑乔就大惑不解，对蒋一轮说："这不大可能。"那天，桑乔站在正在写大字的纸月身后，一直看她将一张纸写完，然后从心底里认定："这孩子的坐相、握笔与运笔，绝对是有规矩与讲究的，不可能是天生的。"后来，桑乔又从蒋一轮那里得知：这个小纸月还会背许多古诗词。现在语文课本上选的那些古诗词，她是早就会了的，并且还很会朗诵。蒋一轮还将纸月写的作文拿给桑乔看了，桑乔直觉得那作文虽然还是一番童趣，但在字面底下，却有一般孩子根本不可能有的灵气与书卷气。所有这一切，都让桑乔十分纳闷。他询问过板仓小学的老师，板仓小学的老师也说不出个所以然来。

不过，桑乔心里倒是暗暗高兴：油麻地小学收了这么一个不错的女孩子。

yet spoken with Sang Sang yet, whom she had met ahead of all the others. Sang Sang didn't take the initiative to speak with her, either. But it was OK. Zhi Yue was happy in Youmadi. A rosy complexion came to her slightly pale face.

Soon, the students learned that Zhi Yue was in fact an amazing girl. Her brush writing was the best in the school. Jiang Yilun circled almost every character of hers in red, as a way of showing admiration. Sang Qiao's brush writing was the best among all teachers. When he saw Zhi Yue's exercise book, he commented, "The child's writing is beautiful, not aggressive; not hasty. She must have been guided by someone." He got Jiang Yilun to call Zhi Yue over and asked, "Who taught you to write?" Zhi Yue said, "Nobody taught me." Sang Qiao was bewildered. He said to Jiang Yilun, "This is impossible." The other day, Sang Qiao stood behind Zhi Yue, who was writing with a brush. He looked at her until she completed a whole page. Sang Qiao simply knew. "The way she sat, held and applied the brush is definitely the result of good training. She was not born with it." Later, Sang Qiao learned from Jiang Yilun that little Zhi Yue had memorized many ancient poems and prose. She had learned long ago the few ancient poems and prose in the textbooks; she was able to recite them all. Jiang Yilun showed Zhi Yue's compositions to Sang Qiao. Sang Qiao thought that although they were immature, there was some sort of thinking and inspiration behind them which didn't seem to belong to a child. Sang Qiao was puzzled by all these things. He inquired of the teachers of Bancang Primary School, but they had no clue either.

Sang Qiao was secretly quite happy. Youmadi Primary School had admitted a brilliant girl.

纸月却没有一点点傲气。她居然丝毫也不觉得她比其他孩子有什么高出的地方，一副平平常常的样子。她让油麻地小学的老师们居然觉得，她大概一辈子都会是一个文弱、恬静、清纯而柔和的女孩儿。

桑桑觉得很难说纸月就没有对他说过话。只不过是她没有用嘴说，而是用眼睛说罢了。比如说桑桑在课桌上再架课桌，又架课桌，最后还加了一张小凳，然后玩杂技一样颤颤抖抖地爬到最顶端，到高墙的洞中掏麻雀时，纸月见了，就仰着脸，两手抱着拳放在下巴下，眼睛睁得大大的，满是紧张与担忧。这时，桑桑假如看到了这双眼睛，就会听出："桑桑，你下来吧，下来吧。"再比如说桑桑顺手从地里拔了根胡萝卜，在袖子上搓擦了几下，就咯吱咯吱地吃起来时，纸月见了，就会令人觉察不到地皱一下眉头，嘴微微地张着看了一眼桑桑。这时，桑桑假如看到了这双眼睛，就会听出："桑桑，不洗的萝卜也是吃得的吗？"再比如说桑桑把时间玩光了，来不及去抠算术题了，打算将邻桌的作业本抓过来抄一通时，纸月看见了，就会把眼珠转到眼角上来看桑桑。这时，假如桑桑看到了这双眼睛，就会听出："桑桑，这样的事也是做得的吗？"又比如说桑桑与人玩篮球，在被对方狠咬了一口，胳膊上都流出鲜血来了，也没有将手中的球松掉，还坚持将它投到篮筐里时，纸月看见了，就会用细白的牙齿咬住薄薄的、血色似有似无的嘴唇，弯曲的双眉下，眼睛在阳光下跳着亮点。这时，假如桑桑看到了这双眼睛，就会听出："桑桑，你真了不起！"

Zhi Yue wasn't arrogant at all. She didn't feel she was superior to other kids in any way. She presented herself as an ordinary girl. Teachers all felt she would be a gentle, frail, quiet, pure and soft girl all her life.

Sang Sang felt it was hard to say whether Zhi Yue had spoken with him or not. Perhaps she didn't speak with her mouth but with her eyes. For example, when Sang Sang laid a desk upon a desk, added another desk, then a stool, and climbed to the very top as if playing circus, and searched for sparrows in the hole in the high wall, Zhi Yue would raise her face, her hands crossed under her chin, eyes wide open, looking nervous and concerned. If Sang Sang saw her eyes, he would actually be hearing, "Sang Sang, come down, please." When Sang Sang picked a carrot from the field, wiped it casually on his sleeve and ate it, Zhi Yue would knit her brows indistinctly, open her mouth slightly and glimpse at Sang Sang. If Sang Sang saw her eyes, he would be hearing, "Sang Sang, how can you eat an unwashed carrot?" When Sang Sang wasted his time and forgot his math problem sets, and intended to copy the exercise book of the boy sharing a desk with him, Zhi Yue would look at Sang Sang from the corner of her eyes. If Sang Sang saw her eyes, he would hear, "Sang Sang, how can you do such a thing?" One day, when Sang Sang was playing d basketball, he was bitten hard by an opponent. Blood dripped from his arm. But Sang Sang didn't drop his ball -- he kept going and shot the ball into the basket. Zhi Yue bit her thin, pale lips with her fine, white teeth. Under her curved brows, her eyes lit up under the sun. If Sang Sang had seen her eyes, he would have heard, "Sang Sang, you are great!"

这些日子，吃饭没有吃相，走路没有走相，难得安静的桑桑，似乎多了几分柔和。桑桑的母亲很纳闷，终于在见到桑桑吃饭不再吃得桌上汤汤水水，直到将碗里最后一颗米粒也拨进嘴里才去看他的鸽子时，向桑桑的父亲感叹道："我们家桑桑，怎么变得文雅起来了?"

这时，正将饭吃得桌上汤汤水水的妹妹柳柳，向母亲大声说："哥哥不再抢我的饼吃了。"

3

初冬的一天下午，北风越刮越大，到了快放学时，天气迅捷阴沉下来。桑桑家的那些在外觅食的鸽子，受了惊吓，立即离开野地，飞上乱云飞渡的天空，然后像被大风吹得乱飘的枯叶一般，飘飘忽忽地飞回草房子。白杨在大风里呜响，旗杆上的麻绳一下一下猛烈地鞭打着旗杆，发出叭叭的声响。孩子们兴奋而略带恐怖地坐在教室里，早已听不下去课，只在心里想着：怎么回家去呢？桑乔走出办公室，呛了几口北风，系好领扣，看了看眼看就要压到头上的天空，便跑到各个教室说："现在就放学！"

不一会儿，各个教室的门都打开了，孩子们只管将书本与文具胡乱地塞进书包，叫喊着，或互相呼唤着同路者的名

These days, Sang Sang, who was rarely quiet, who didn't eat or walk properly, seemed to have mellowed. His mother was puzzled. When she saw that Sang Sang didn't make a mess on the table with water and soup and finished the last bit of rice before going to see his pigeons, the mother sighed to the father, "How is it that Sang Sang has become so good-mannered?

Sister Liu Liu, who was making a mess on the table with water and soup, said to her mother in a loud voice, "Elder brother doesn't fight for my round flat cake anymore."

3

One afternoon in early winter, the north wind blew more and more strongly. When class was almost over, it was rapidly starting to get dark. Sang Sang's pigeons, looking for food outside, were startled. They left the wild fields quickly, flew to the sky with the rampant clouds, and then back to the straw house like withered leaves blown by the strong wind. White poplars rustled in the strong wind. The flax rope tied to the flagpole whipped it hard, again and again, making a smacking sound. Children sat in the classrooms, excited and fearful. Their minds were far away. They were thinking: how can I get home? Sang Qiao walked out of the classroom and was choked by the north wind. He tightened his collar, glanced at the sky, and ran to each classroom: "Class is over now."

Soon the classroom doors were all open. Children hurriedly put their textbooks, exercise books and stationery into their bags. They shouted, called the names of others who would go

字，纷纷往校园外面跑，仿佛马上就有一场劫难。

纸月收拾好自己的书包时，教室里就只剩她一个人了。她朝门外看了看，一脸的惶恐与不安。因为，她马上想到了：不等她回到家中，半路上就会有暴风雨的。那时，前不着村后不着店，她可怎么办呢？

桑桑的母亲正在混乱的孩子群中朝这边走着，见着站在风中打哆嗦的桑桑问："纸月呢？"

桑桑："在教室里。"

桑桑的母亲急忙走到教室门口："纸月。"

纸月见了桑桑的母亲，学着外婆的叫法，叫了一声："师娘。"

"你今天不要回家了。"

"外婆在等我呢。"

"我已托人带信给你外婆了。跟我回家去。天马上就要下雨了。"

纸月说："我还是回家吧。"

桑桑的母亲说："你会被雨浇在半路上的。"说罢，就过来拉住纸月冰凉的手："走吧，外婆那边肯定会知道的。"

当纸月跟着桑桑的母亲走出教室时，纸月不知为什么低下了头，眼睛里汪了泪水。

一直在不远处站着的桑桑，见母亲领着纸月正往这边走赶紧回头先回家了。

纸月来到桑桑家不久，天就下起雨来，一开头就很猛烈。

on the same path, and ran outside the school, as if a disaster were looming.

When Zhi Yue tidied up her desk, she was the only one left in the classroom. She took a look outside and was full of anxiety and unease. She knew there would be a thunderstorm before she got home. What should she do?

Sang Sang's mother walked over through the chaotic crowd. She saw Sang Sang shaking in the wind and asked, "Where is Zhi Yue?"

Sang Sang said, "In the classroom."

Sang Sang's mother hurried to the classroom, "Zhi Yue."

Zhi Yue saw Sang Sang's mother, and called "Madam Sang," the way her grandmother addressed Sang Sang's mother.

"Don't you go home today. Stay with us."

"Grandmother is waiting for me."

"I have asked someone to pass the news to your grandmother. Go home with me. It is going to rain."

Zhi Yue said, "I'd better go home."

Sang Sang's mother said, "You will be trapped in the rain on your way." She came over and pulled the cold hand of Zhi Yue's. "Come with me -- your grandmother will know where you are."

When Zhi Yue followed Sang Sang's mother out of the classroom, she lowered her head for no reason at all; tears filled her eyes.

Sang Sang had been standing not far way. He saw his mother walking with Zhi Yue, and went back home immediately.

It began to rain as soon as Zhi Yue arrived at Sang Sang's. It was heavy from the very beginning. Sang Sang leaned against

桑桑趴在窗台上往外看时，只见四下里白茫茫的一片，油麻地小学的草房子在雨幕里都看不成形了，虚虚幻幻的。

柳柳听说纸月要在她家过夜，异常兴奋，拉住纸月的手就不肯再松开，反复向母亲说："我跟纸月姐姐睡一张床。"

纸月的神情不一会儿就安定自如了。

在柳柳与纸月说话，纸月被柳柳拉着在屋里不住地走动时，桑桑在一旁不住地给两只小鸽子喂食。忙着做晚饭的母亲，在弥漫于灶房里的雾气中说："你是非要把这两只小鸽子撑死不可。"

桑桑这才不喂鸽子。可是桑桑不知道做什么好。他只好又趴到窗台上去，望望外面：天已晚了，黑乎乎的，那些草房子已几乎看不见了。但桑桑通过檐口的雨滴声，至少可以判断出离他家最近的那两幢草房子的位置。桑桑的耳朵里，除了稠密的雨声，偶尔会穿插进来柳柳与纸月的说笑声。

隐隐约约地，从屋后的大河上，传来打鱼人因为天气不好而略带些悲伤的歌声。

纸月果然被桑桑的母亲安排和柳柳睡一张床。柳柳便脱了鞋，爬到床上高兴地蹦跳。母亲就说："柳柳别闹。"柳柳却蹦得更高。

母亲及时地在屋子中央烧了一个大火盆。屋外虽是凉风冷雨，但这草房子里，却是暖融融的。柳柳与纸月的脸颊被暖得红红的。

the windowsill and looked outside. It was a vast expanse of whiteness. The straw houses of Youmadi Primary School were shapeless in the curtain of rain, only half visible.

When Liu Liu heard Zhi Yue was to spend the night at her home, she was very excited. She grabbed Zhi Yue's hand and wouldn't let go. She repeated to her mother, "I'll sleep with Zhi Yue sister."

Zhi Yue soon felt quite comfortable.

Liu Liu chatted with Zhi Yue and pulled her all over the house. Sang Sang kept on feeding two little pigeons. His mother was busy cooking. In the steamy air of the kitchen, she called, "You will stuff the pigeons to death if you feed them like that."

Sang Sang stopped, but he didn't know what to do. He leaned against the windowsill again and looked outside. It was late and dark and the straw houses were invisible now. By the sound of falling rain from the eaves, Sang Sang could still tell the location of the two straw houses nearest home. Apart from the sound of the dense rain, Sang Sang could also hear Liu Liu and Zhi Yue's chattering and occasional laughter.

From the big river behind the house, the sorrowful ballads of fishermen came over half-audibly. They were lamenting their loss of business because of the rain.

Sang Sang's mother put Zhi Yue and Liu Liu in the same bed. Liu Liu took off her shoes, and jumped happily on the bed. Her mother said, "Liu Liu, stop." Liu Liu jumped even higher.

The mother set up a big heating pan in the middle of the room. There was only cold wind and rain outside, but the straw house was warm. Liu Liu and Zhi Yue's cheeks reddened.

在睡前忙碌的母亲，有时会停住看一眼纸月。她的目光里，总是含着一份丢不下的怜爱。

桑桑睡在里间，纸月和柳柳睡在外间。里间与外间，隔了一道薄薄的用芦苇秆编成的篱笆。因此，外间柳柳与纸月的说话声，桑桑都听得十分分明——

纸月教柳柳一句一句地念着：

一树黄梅个个青，
打雷落雨满天星。
三个和尚四方坐，
不言不语口念经。

柳柳一边念一边乐得咯咯笑。学完了，又缠着纸月再念一个。纸月很乐意：

正月梅花香又香，
二月兰花盆里装。
三月桃花红十里，
四月蔷薇靠短墙。
五月石榴红似火，
六月荷花满池塘。
七月栀子头上戴，
八月桂花满树黄。
九月菊花初开放，
十月芙蓉正上妆。
十一月水仙供上案，
十二月腊梅雪里香。

The busy mother glanced at Zhi Yue occasionally. Her eyes were full of affection.

Sang Sang slept in the inner room, Zhi Yue and Liu Liu in the outer room. There was a thin fence made of reed stalks separating the two rooms. Sang Sang could hear clearly Liu Liu and Zhi Yue's conversation.

Zhi Yue was teaching a ballad to Liu Liu.

There was a tree of green plums, each very green,
When it was thundering and raining, stars filled the sky.
Three monks sat in a square,
In silence, they recited their sutra.

Liu Liu recited it and giggled. She asked Zhi Yue for another. Zhi Yue was happy to teach her.

In the first month of lunar year, Chinese plum flowers smell good,
In February, orchids are aplenty in pans.
In March, peach blossoms are red for 10 li,
In April, roses lean against short walls.
In May, pomegranates are red as fire,
In June, lotuses fill the pond.
In July, gardenias are worn in the hair,
In August, yellow osmanthus flowers blossom on trees.
In September, chrysanthemums begin to blossom,
In October, cottonrose hibiscus is flourishing.
In November, narcissus is put on the table,
In December, wintersweet diffuses aroma in snow.

桑桑睁着一双大眼，也在心里默默地念着。

母亲将一切收拾停当，在里屋叫道：“柳柳，别再总缠着姐姐了，天不早了，该睡觉了。”

灯一盏一盏地相继熄灭。

两个女孩在一条被窝里睡着，大概是互相碰着了，不住地咯咯地笑。过不一会儿，柳柳说：“纸月姐姐，我和你一头睡行吗？”

纸月说：“你过来吧。”

柳柳就像一只猫似的从被窝里爬了过来。当柳柳终于钻到纸月怀里时，两个女孩又是一阵咯咯咯的笑。

就听见里屋里母亲说了一句：“柳柳疯死了。”

柳柳赶紧闭嘴，直往纸月怀里乱钻着。但过不一会儿，桑桑就又听见柳柳跟纸月说话。这回声音小，好像是两个人都钻到被窝里去了。但桑桑依然还是隐隐约约地听清了——是柳柳在向纸月讲他的坏话——

柳柳：“好多年前，好多年前，我哥哥……”

纸月：“怎么会好多年前呢？”

柳柳：“反正有好几年了。那天，我哥哥把家里的一口锅拿到院子里，偷偷地砸了。”

纸月：“砸锅干什么？”

柳柳：“卖铁换钱呗。”

纸月：“换钱干什么？”

柳柳：“换钱买鸽子呗。”

纸月：“后来呢？”

Sang Sang opened his eyes wide and recited the ballad silently in his heart.

His mother finished her chores and called, "Liu Liu, don't bother sister anymore. It is late and time to sleep."

Lights were put out one by one.

The two girls shared one quilt. Perhaps they touched each other and kept on giggling. After a while, Liu Liu said, "Zhi Yue sister, can I sleep on the same end with you?"

Zhi Yue said, "Sure, come over."

Liu Liu climbed to Zhi Yue's end like a cat. When she crawled into Zhi Yue's embrace, the two girls giggled again.

The mother said, "Liu Liu gets crazy."

Liu Liu kept quiet and joyfully held Zhi Yue's embrace. After a while, Sang Sang heard them talking again. The voice was very low, as if both girls had sneaked under the quilt. But Sang Sang still heard part of their conversation. Liu Liu was saying bad things about him.

Liu Liu: "Many years ago, my brother..."

Zhi Yue: "Many years ago?"

Liu Liu: "At least several years ago, my brother secretly broke a pan in the courtyard."

Zhi Yue: "Why did he do that?"

Liu Liu: "He wanted to sell the iron for money."

Zhi Yue: "Why did he want the money?"

Liu Liu: "To buy pigeons."

Zhi Yue: "What happened later?"

柳柳："后来妈妈烧饭，发现锅没有了，就找锅，到处找不着，就问哥哥看见锅没有，哥哥看着妈妈就往后退。妈妈明白了，就要去抓住哥哥……"

纸月："他跑了吗？"

柳柳："跑了。"

纸月："跑哪儿啦？"

柳柳："院门正好关着呢，他跑不了，就爬到猪圈里去了。"

纸月："爬到猪圈里去了？"

柳柳："爬到猪圈里去了。老母猪就哼哼哼地要过来咬他。"

纸月有点紧张："咬着了吗？"

柳柳："哥哥踩了一脚猪屎，又爬出来了……"

纸月躲在被窝里笑了。

柳柳："我哥可脏啦。他早上不洗脸就吃饭！"

桑桑听得咬牙切齿，恨不能从床上蹦下来，一把将柳柳从热烘烘的被窝里抓出来，然后踢她一脚。

幸好，柳柳渐渐困了，又糊里糊涂说了几句，就搂着纸月的脖子睡着了。

不一会儿，桑桑就听到了两个女孩细弱而均匀的鼾声。

窗外，雨还在淅沥淅沥地下着。有只鸽子，大概是被雨打湿了，咕咕叫着，但想到这也是很平常的事，叫了两声，也就不叫了。

桑桑不久也睡着了。

后半夜，风停了，雨停了，天居然在飘散了三两团乌云

Liu Liu: "Mum was cooking but couldn't find the pan. She looked for it everywhere but couldn't find it. She asked brother whether he saw it. Brother looked at mum and retreated backward. Mum realized what happened and grabbed brother..."

Zhi Yue: "Did he run away?"

Liu Liu: "Yes."

Zhi Yue: "Where to?"

Liu Liu: "The door of the courtyard was closed. He had nowhere to go. So he went to the pigpen."

Zhi Yue: "To the pigpen?"

Liu Liu: "Yes indeed. The old sow was about to bite him."

Zhi Yue was nervous. "Was he bitten?"

Liu Liu: "No, he stepped on the dung and climbed out..."

Zhi Yue hid in the quilt and laughed.

Liu Liu: "My brother is really dirty. He has breakfast before washing!"

Sang Sang clenched his teeth. He desperately wanted to pull Liu Liu out from under her warm quilt and kick her.

Fortunately, Liu Liu gradually became sleepy. She mumbled something, held Zhi Yue's neck and went to sleep.

After a while, Sang Sang heard the gentle and even breathing of the two girls.

It was still raining outside the window. A pigeon, perhaps getting wet in the rain, was loudly cooing. It was not unusual. After a couple of cries, it stopped.

Sang Sang soon went to sleep.

Halfway through the night, the wind and rain stopped.

之后，出来了月亮。

夜行的野鸭，疲倦了，就往大河里落。落到水面上，大概是因为大鱼好奇地吸吮了它们的脚，惊得呱呱一阵叫。

桑桑醒来了。桑桑的第一个念头就是想撒尿，但桑桑不能撒尿。因为桑桑想到自己如果要撒尿，就必须从里间走出，然后穿过外间走到门外去，而从外间走过时，必须要经过纸月的床前。桑桑只好忍着。他感觉到自己的小肚子正越来越严重地鼓胀起来。他有点懊悔晚上不该喝下那么多汤的。可是当时，他只想头也不抬地喝。幸亏就那么多汤，如果盆里有更多的汤，这下就更糟糕了。桑桑不想一个劲地想着撒尿，就让自己去想点其他的事情。他想到了住在校园里的秦大奶奶：现在，她是睡着呢，还是醒着呢？听父母亲说，她一个人过了一辈子。这么长的夜晚，就她一个人，不觉得孤单吗？他又想到了油麻地第一富庶人家的儿子杜小康。他在心里说：你傲什么？你有什么好傲的？但桑桑又不免悲哀地承认一年四季总是穿着白球鞋的杜小康，确实是其他孩子不能比的——他的样子，他的成绩，还有很多很多方面，都是不能和他比的。桑桑突然觉得，杜小康傲，是有理由的。但桑桑依然不服气，甚至很生气……

小肚的胀痛，打断了桑桑的思路。

桑桑忽然听到了纸月于梦中发出的叹气声。于是桑桑又去很混乱地想纸月：纸月从田埂上走过来的样子，纸月读书

The moon came out behind two or three clumps of dark clouds.

Wild ducks traveling in the night were tired and descended on the surface of the big river. They screamed; perhaps their feet were being nibbled by some big fishs, out of curiosity.

Sang Sang woke up. The first thought that came to him was to pee. But he couldn't. He had to walk out of his room, past Zhi Yue's bed in the outer room. So he held it. He felt his underbelly was swelling rather seriously. He regretted a bit having had so much soup in the evening. At dinnertime, he had just wanted to keep his head low and drink soup. Thank goodness there was just so much soup. If there had been more, his condition would have been worse. Sang Sang tried to think of something else rather than peeing, so he thought of Granny Qin living at the school. Was she asleep or awake now? His parents said she had spent her whole life on her own. Such a long night -- was she alone? Sang Sang also thought of Du Xiaokang, the son of the richest family in Youmadi. He asked to himself, why are you so arrogant? But he had to admit sadly that Du Xiaokang, who always wore white sneakers in all four seasons, was the one and only. The way he looked, his academic performance, and many other things -- nobody could compare with him. Sang Sang acknowledged that Du Xiaokang had reasons to be arrogant. But Sang Sang wasn't happy; he was even angry...

The swelling pain from his underbelly interrupted his thoughts.

Sang Sang suddenly heard Zhi Yue sighing in her dreams. His chaotic thoughts went to Zhi Yue: how she looked walking from the low bank between the fields; the sound she made

的声音，纸月的毛笔字，纸月在舞台上舞着大红绸……

后来，桑桑又睡着了。

第二天早上，母亲在收拾桑桑的床时，手突然感觉到了潮湿，打开被子一看，发现桑桑夜里尿床了。她很惊诧：桑桑还是五岁前尿过床，怎么现在十多岁了又尿床了？她一边将被子抱到院子里晾着，一边在心里犯嘀咕。

早晨的阳光十分明亮地照着桑桑的被子。

温幼菊进了院子，见了晾在绳子上的被，问："是谁呀？"

母亲说："是桑桑。"

那时，纸月正背着书包从屋里出来。但纸月只看了一眼那床被子，就走出了院子。

桑桑一头跑进了屋子。

过了一刻钟，桑桑出来了，见院子里无人，将被子狠狠地从绳子上扯下来，扔到了地上。而当时的地上，还留着夜间的积水。

母亲正好出来看到了，望着已走出院门的桑桑："你找死哪！"

桑桑猛地扭过头来看了母亲一眼，抹了一把眼泪，跑掉了。

4

这天，纸月没有来上学。她的外婆来油麻地小学请假，

while reading, her brush writing; the way she had danced in big red silk on the stage...

Sang Sang went back to sleep.

The next morning, when the mother made up Sang Sang's bed, she felt moisture. She opened his quilt and saw that Sang Sang had wet his bed. She was very surprised: Sang Sang had wet before he was five. But now he was more than ten -- how could he wet again? She thought about it while taking the quilt to the courtyard to dry.

The morning sunshine shone brightly on Sang Sang's quilt.

Wen Youju walked into the courtyard. She saw the quilt drying on the rope and asked, "Whose is it?"

The mother said, "Sang Sang's."

Zhi Yue walked out from the room carrying her bag. She just glanced at the quilt before walking to school.

Sang Sang ran into the room.

After fifteen minutes, Sang Sang came out. When he saw there was nobody in the courtyard, he grabbed the quilt from the rope and threw it to the ground. There was still water from the previous night on the ground.

His mother saw it and scolded Sang Sang, who walked out of the courtyard, "Darn you!"

Sang Sang turned abruptly and looked at his mother. He wiped his tears and ran away.

4

One day, Zhi Yue didn't come to school. Her grandmother

说纸月生病了。纸月差不多有一个星期没有来上学。蒋一轮看看纸月落下了许多作业，就对桑桑说：“你跑一趟板仓，将作业本给纸月带上，把老师布置的题告诉她，看她能不能在家把作业补了。”

桑桑点头答应了，但桑桑不愿一个人去，就拉了阿恕一起去。可是走到半路上，遇到了阿恕的母亲，硬把阿恕留下了，说她家的鸭子不知游到什么地方去了，让阿恕去找鸭子。桑桑犹豫了一阵，就只好独自一人往板仓走。

桑桑想象着纸月生病的样子。但天空飞过一群鸽子，他就仰脸去望。他把那群鸽子一只一只地数了。他见了人家的鸽群，总要数一数。若发现人家的鸽群大于他的鸽群，他就有些小小的嫉妒；若发现人家的鸽群小于他的鸽群，他就有些小小的得意。现在，头上的这个鸽群是小于他的鸽群的，他就笑了，并且蹦起来，去够头上的树枝，结果把纸月的作业本震落了一地。他只好蹲下来收拾作业本，并把作业本上的灰擦去。鸽群还在他头上飞，他沉浸在得意感里，早把纸月忘了。

离板仓大约一里地，有条大河。大河边上有一大片树林，在林子深处，有一座古寺，叫浸月寺。鸽群早已消失了，桑桑一边走，一边想那座古寺。他和母亲一起来过这座古寺。桑桑想：我马上就要见到那座古寺了。

came to ask for leave for her, saying she was sick. Zhi Yue didn't come for almost a week. Jiang Yilun saw that she had left a lot of homework undone, so he asked Sang Sang, "You go to Bancang, take the exercise books to Zhi Yue; give her the problem sets given by the teachers and see whether she can do them at home."

Sang Sang nodded, but he didn't want to go by himself. He asked A Xu to go with him. On their way, they met A Xu's mother, who made him stay. She said their duck was missing, and asked A Xu to go and to look for the duck. Sang Sang hesitated, but went on by himself.

Sang Sang imagined the sick Zhi Yue. A flock of pigeons flew past, and he raised his head to watch. He counted the number in the flock. Each time he saw a flock of pigeons, he would count the number. If he found it was more than his own, he would be a bit envious; on the contrary, if they were fewer, he would be a bit smug. Now he smiled, because this flock was smaller than his. He jumped and touched the branches above his head. He dropped Zhi Yue's exercise books all over the ground. He had to squat and pick them up, and wipe the dust off. The flock of pigeons were still flying up. Sang Sang, feeling conceited, for a moment forgot Zhi Yue.

He came to a big river approximately one li away from Bancang. There was a big stretch of forest by the river. And there was an old temple in the depth of the forest called Jin Yue (immersing moon) Temple. The pigeons had gone, and Sang Sang thought of the old temple. He had been here with his mother. Sang Sang thought, I am going to see the old temple now.

桑桑走到了大河边，不一会儿，就见到了那片林子。不知为什么，桑桑并不想立即见到纸月。因为他不知道自己在见了纸月以后，会是什么样子。桑桑是一个与女孩子说话就会脸红的男孩。越走近板仓，他就越磨蹭起来。他走进了林子，想看看浸月寺以后再说。有一条青石板的小道，弯弯曲曲地隐藏在林子间，把桑桑往林子深处引着。

正在冬季里，所有的树，无论是枫树、白杨还是银杏，都赤条条的。风并不大，但林子还是呼呼呼地响着，渲染着冬季的萧条。几只寒鸦立在晃动的枝头，歪脸看着天空那轮冬季特有的太阳。

浸月寺立在坡上。

桑桑先听到浸月寺风铃的清音，随即看到了它的一角。风铃声渐渐大起来。桑桑觉得这风铃声很神秘，很奇妙，也很好听。他想：如果有一种鸽哨，也能发出这种声音，从天空中飘过，那会怎样呢？桑桑的许多想法，最后都是要与他的那群鸽子汇合到一起去。

拐了一道弯，浸月寺突然整个放在了桑桑的眼前。

立在深院里的寺庙，四角翘翘，仿佛随时都会随风飞去。寺庙后面还是林子，有三两株高树，在它的背后露出枝条来。寺前是两株巨大的老槐，很少枝条，而偶尔剩下的几

Sang Sang walked to the riverside and immediately saw the forest. He didn't know why, but he didn't want to see Zhi Yue just now. He didn't know how he would behave when he saw her. Sang Sang's face always turned red when he talked with girls. The closer he approached Bancang, the slower he became. He walked into the forest, planning to see the temple first. There was a little path paved with blue stone plates, winding and hidden in the trees, leading Sang Sang to the depth of the forest.

It was winter; all the trees, Chinese sweet gums, white poplars and ginkgos were bare. The wind wasn't too strong, but the forest was still rustling, adding to the barrenness of winter. A few jackdaws stood on the shaking branches, tilting their heads to face the sun in the winter sky.

Jin Yue temple was on a slope.

Sang Sang first heard the aeolian bell ringing in the temple, then saw a corner of the temple. The sound of the bell got louder. Sang Sang felt it was mysterious and magical, and pleasant-sounding. He thought, if there were a kind of pigeon cry making a sound like that and floating across the air, wouldn't it be wonderful? Sang Sang's numerous ideas always had something to do his pigeons.

Sang Sang turned a corner and the whole of Jin Yue temple was in front of his eyes.

In a deep courtyard, the temple stood with four raised corners, as if it could fly away anytime with the wind. There was a forest behind the temple. Branches of a couple of tall trees stretched behind the temple. There were two gigantic old Chinese scholar trees in front of the temple with very few

根，在风中轻轻摇动，显得十分苍劲。风略大一些，四角垂挂的风铃一起响起，丁丁当当，衬得四周更是寂静。

独自一人来到寺前的桑桑，忽然觉得被一种肃穆与庄严压迫着，不禁打了一个寒噤，小小的身体收缩住，惶惶不安地望着，竟不敢再往前走了。

“往回走吧，去纸月家。”桑桑对自己说。但他并未往回走，反而往上走来了。这时，桑桑听到老槐树下传来了三弦的弹拨声。桑桑认得这种乐器。弹拨三弦的人，似乎很安静，三弦声始终不急躁，十分单纯。在桑桑听来，这声音是单调的，并且是重复的。但桑桑又觉得它这清纯的、缓慢的声音是好听的，像秋天雨后树枝上的雨滴落在池塘里那么好听。桑桑是油麻地小学文艺宣传队的胡琴手，桑桑多少懂得一点音乐。

三弦声总是这么响着。仿佛在许多许多年前，它就响了，就这么响的。它还会永远响下去，就这么地响下去。

桑桑终于怯怯地走到了寺院门口。他往里一看，见一个僧人正坐在老槐树下。那三弦正在他怀里似有似无地响着。

桑桑知道，这就是父亲常常说起的慧思和尚。

关于慧思和尚的身世，这一带人有多种说法。但桑桑的父亲只相信一种：这个人从前是个教书先生，并且是一个很有学问的教书先生，后来也不知是什么原因，突然出家当和

branches. The few remaining branches vibrated lightly in the wind, looking strong. The wind rose. Aeolian bells hung on the four corners rang at the same time. But the feeling was of quietude.

Sang Sang, having come to the temple alone, was suddenly enveloped by a feeling of both solemnity and grandeur. He trembled a bit and pulled back. He looked ahead with anxiety, and dared not walk forward.

"Turn back and go to Zhi Yue's," he told himself. But he didn't. Instead, he stepped forward. Sang Sang heard the sound of a three-stringed instrument being strummed. He knew this instrument. The person playing and sweeping it seemed to be serene. The sound was pure and unhurried. It was repetitive, even monotonous, thought Sang Sang. But he also savored this pure and slow sound, like raindrops dropping from branches after rain, to the pond. Sang Sang played the huqin on the Youmadi performance team, so he knew a bit about music.

The music continued, as if it had started many years ago, and it would continue forever, just like that.

Sang Sang finally timidly approached the entrance. He looked inside, and saw a monk sitting under a scholar tree, with a three-stringed instrument clutched to his chest, making real or virtual sounds.

Sang Sang knew he was monk Hui Si (intelligent thinking) -- his father often spoke of him.

There were many tales about monk Hui Si in the neighborhood. But Sang Sang's father believed in only one version. The monk used to be a teacher, and a very learned one. For some unknown reason, he suddenly decided to

尚了。父亲实际并无充足的理由，只是在见过慧思和尚几次之后，从他的一手很好的毛笔字上，从他的一口风雅言辞上，从他的文质彬彬且又带了几分洒脱的举止上，便认定了许多种说法中的这一种。父亲后来也曾怀疑过他是一个念书已念得很高的学生。是先生也好，是学生也罢，反正，慧思和尚不是乡野之人。慧思和尚显然出生于江南，因为只有江南人才有那副清秀之相。慧思和尚是1948年来浸月寺的。据当时的人讲，慧思那时还不足二十岁，头发黑如鸦羽，面白得有点像女孩子，让他的朋友们觉得可惜。后来，这里的和尚老死的老死了，走的走了，就只剩他一个独自守着这座也不知是建于哪年的古寺。因为时代的变迁，浸月寺实际上已很早就不再像从前那样香烟缭绕了，各种佛事也基本上停止。浸月寺终年清静。不知是什么原因，慧思和尚却一直留了下来。这或许是因为他已无处可去，古寺就成了他的家。他坚持着没有还俗，在空寂的岁月中，依然做他的和尚。他像从前一样，一年四季穿着棕色的僧袍。他偶尔出现在田野上，出现在小镇上，这倒给平淡无奇的乡野增添了一道风景。

老槐树下的慧思和尚感觉到有人站在院门口，就抬起头来。

就在这一刹那间，桑桑看到了一双深邃的眼睛。尽管这种目光里含着一种慈祥，但桑桑却像被一股凉风吹着了似的，微微震颤了一下。

become a monk. In fact, Sang Sang's father didn't have any particular reason to believe in this version. But he saw the monk a few times, and was impressed by his beautiful brush writing, his elegant conversation, and his scholarly and unaffected bearing. Sang Sang's father was convinced of his version of the story. He had also guessed the monk might have been a brilliant student. Teacher or student, he was absolutely not a countryside man. The monk was obviously born in the region south of the Yangtze River; only people from there could look so gentle. He had come to the temple in 1948. According to people who were around then, Hui Si was under twenty when he came. His hair was as dark as the feathers of crows, his face as white as a girl. His friends regretted that he had become a monk. Later, other monks either died of old age or left, and there was only Hui Si remaining in a temple whose age nobody was sure. Over time, activities at the temple became fewer, and most Buddhist ceremonies had stopped. It was a very quiet place. For whatever reason, monk Hui Si stayed. Perhaps he had nowhere to go and the temple was his only home. He didn't return to secular life. During the long solitary years, he was still a monk. He always wore a brown gown, all year round. Occasionally he appeared in the fields or in a village, making quite a picture in the mundane settings of the countryside.

Monk Hui Si, sitting under the scholar tree, felt the presence of someone at the entrance. He lifted his head.

At that moment, Sang Sang saw a pair of profound eyes. Although they were kind, he shook a bit as if blown by a gush of cold wind.

慧思和尚轻轻放下三弦，用双手捏住僧袍，然后站起来，轻轻一松手，那僧袍就像一道幕布滑落下去。他用手又轻轻拂了几下僧袍，低头向桑桑作了一个揖，便走了过来。

桑桑不敢看慧思和尚的脸，目光平视。由于个头的差异，桑桑的目光里，是两只摆动的宽大的袖子。那袖子是宽宽地卷起的，露出雪白的里子。

“小施主，请进。”

桑桑壮大了胆抬起头来。他眼前是副充满清爽、文静之气的面孔。桑桑长这么大，还从未见过这样的面孔。他朝慧思和尚笑了笑，但他不知道他这么笑究竟是什么意思，只是觉得自己应该这么笑一笑。

慧思和尚微微弯腰，做了一个很恭敬的、让桑桑进入僧院的动作。

桑桑有点不自然。因为，谁也没有对他这样一个几年前还拖着鼻涕的孩子如此庄重过。

桑桑束手束脚地走进了僧院。

慧思和尚闪在一侧，略微靠前一点引导着桑桑往前走。他问桑桑：“小施主，有什么事吗？”

桑桑随口说：“来玩玩。”但他马上觉得自己的回答很荒唐。因为，这儿不是小孩玩的地方。他的脸一下涨红起来。

然而，慧思和尚并没有对他说“这不是玩的地方”，只是

Monk Hui Si put down his three-stringed instrument, lifted his gown with both hands and stood up. He loosened his hands, and the gown fell down like a curtain. He flicked his gown lightly, lowered his head, bowed to Sang Sang and walked over.

Sang Sang dared not look at his face. He looked straight ahead. Since he was shorter than the monk, he saw only his loose sleeves. The sleeves were rolled up and Sang Sang saw the snow-white lining inside.

"Little patron, please come in."

Sang Sang braved it and raised his head. There was a clean and gentle face in front of him. Sang Sang had never seen a face like that in all his life. He smiled at monk Hui Si. But he didn't know what he was supposed to do. He thought maybe he should just smile.

Monk Hui Si bowed slightly, making a respectful gesture to invite Sang Sang to go into the temple.

Sang Sang felt a bit uneasy. Nobody had even been so gracious to him: he still had a runny nose from a couple of years ago.

He walked in timidly and cautiously.

Monk Hui Si stepped aside, and walked slightly ahead to lead Sang Sang inside. He asked Sang Sang, "Little patron, how may I help you?"

Sang Sang said casually, "I just came to play." He immediately realized it was a ridiculous response, since this was not supposed to be a playground for children. His face turned red.

However, monk Hui Si didn't tell him, "This is not a

很亲切地说："噢，噢……"仍在微微靠前的位置上引导着桑桑。

桑桑不好再退回去，索性硬着头皮往前走。他走到了殿门。里面黑沉沉的。桑桑第一眼看里面时，并没有看到具体的形象，只觉得黑暗里泛着金光。他站在高高的门槛外面，不一会儿就看清了那尊莲座上的佛像。佛的神态庄严却很慈祥。佛的上方，是一个金色的穹顶，于是佛像又显得异常地华贵了。

桑桑仰望佛像时，不知为什么，心里忽然有点惧怕起来，便不由自主地往后退了几步，随即转身就要往院外走。

慧思和尚连忙跟了出来。

在桑桑走出院门时，慧思和尚问了一句："小施主从哪儿来？"

桑桑答道："从油麻地。"

慧思和尚又问道："小施主，往哪儿去？"

桑桑答道："去板仓。"

"板仓？"

桑桑点点头："我去板仓找纸月。"

"纸月？"

"我的同学纸月。"

"你是桑桑？"

桑桑很吃惊："你怎么知道我是桑桑？"

慧思和尚顿了一下，然后一笑道："听人说起过，桑校长的公子叫桑桑。你说你是从油麻地来的，我想，你莫非就是桑桑。"

桑桑沿着青石板小道，往回走去。

playground". He said kindly, "Oh..." and still walked slightly ahead to lead Sang Sang in.

Sang Sang felt it wasn't proper to retreat -- he should go on. He walked into the temple. It was dark. At first glance, he didn't see anything, just the golden light in the darkness. He stood outside the high threshold, and immediately saw the Buddha statue on the lotus seat. The Buddha appeared grand and kind. There was a golden ceiling above the Buddha, making the Buddha look extremely lavish.

Sang Sang raised his head to look at the Buddha. He didn't know why, but he was suddenly afraid. He couldn't help himself and retreated a few steps. He turned quickly to walk out of the temple.

As Sang Sang started to leave the temple, monk Hui Si asked, "Where are you from?"

Sang Sang answered, "Youmadi."

Monk Hui Si asked again, "Where are you going?"

Sang Sang answered, "Bancang."

"Bancang?"

Sang Sang nodded, "I'm going to look for Zhi Yue."

"Zhi Yue?"

"My classmate Zhi Yue."

"Are you Sang Sang?"

Sang Sang was very surprised, "How do you know?"

Monk Hui Si paused and smiled, "I heard principal Sang had a son Sang Sang. You said you came from Youmadi. I thought, could you be Sang Sang?"

Sang Sang went back along the blue stone plates-paved path.

慧思和尚竟然一定要送桑桑。

桑桑无法拒绝。桑桑也不知道如何拒绝，就呆头呆脑地让慧思和尚一直将他送到大河边。

“慢走了。”慧思和尚说。

桑桑转过身来看着慧思和尚。当时，太阳正照着大河，河水反射着明亮的阳光，把站在河边草地上的慧思和尚的脸照得非常清晰。慧思和尚也正望着他，朝他微笑。桑桑望着慧思和尚的脸，凭他一个孩子的感觉，他突然无端地觉得，他的眼睛似乎像另外一个人的眼睛，反过来说，有另外一个人的眼睛，似乎像慧思和尚的眼睛。但桑桑却想不出这另外一个人是谁，一脸的困惑。

慧思和尚说：“小施主，过了河，就是板仓了，上路吧。”

桑桑这才将疑惑的目光收住，朝慧思和尚摆摆手，与他告别。

桑桑走出去一大段路以后，又回过头来看。他看到慧思和尚还站在河边的草地上。有大风从河上吹来，他的僧袍被风所卷动，像空中飘动的云一样。

5

纸月病好之后，又像往常一样上学、回家。但这样过了两个星期之后，不知道是什么原因，纸月几乎每天上学迟到。有时，上午的第一节课都快结束了，她才气喘吁吁地赶到教

Monk Hui Si insisted on seeing him off.

Sang Sang didn't know how to refuse. He couldn't say no. In a reverie, he allowed monk Hui Si to accompany him to the riverside.

"Take care," said monk Hui Si.

Sang Sang turned to look at monk Hui Si. The sun shone on the river, which reflected its bright rays, and on the face of monk Hui Si, who stood on the grass near the river. Monk Hui Si looked at Sang Sang and smiled at him. His face was clear. Sang Sang looked at his face. By a child's instinct, he suddenly felt for no reason at all that this pair of eyes looked like that of another person. Someone else's eyes were like his. Sang Sang couldn't think who the person was. He was full of bewilderment.

Monk Hui Si said, "Little patron, when you cross the river, you will be at Bancang. Go."

Sang Sang put aside his thoughts of the monk's eyes. He waved to monk Hui Si and said good-bye to him.

After walking some distance, he turned back to have another look. He saw monk Hui Si still standing on the grass near the river. A big wind blew from the river; his gown was billowing and rolling up, like the drifting wind in the sky.

5

Zhi Yue recovered and came to school and went home as usual. After two weeks, for some reason, she was late almost daily. One day, she rushed into the classroom, nearly out of

室门口，举着手喊“报告”。开始几回，蒋一轮也没有觉得什么，只是说：“进来。”这样的情况又发生了几次之后，蒋一轮有点生气了：“纸月，你是怎么搞的?怎么天天迟到?”

纸月就把头垂了下来。

“以后注意。到座位上去吧!”蒋广轮说。

纸月依然垂着头。纸月坐下之后，就一直垂着头。

有一回，桑桑偶然瞥了纸月一眼，只见有一串泪珠从纸月的脸上无声地滚落了下来，滴在了课本上。

这一天，桑桑起了个大早，对母亲说是有一只鸽子昨晚未能归巢，怕是被鹰打伤了翅膀，他得到田野上去找一找，就跑出了家门。桑桑一出家门就直奔板仓。桑桑想暗暗地搞清楚纸月到底是怎么了。

桑桑赶到大河边时，太阳刚刚出来，河上的雾气正在飘散。河上有一条渡船，两头都拴着绳子，分别连结着两岸。桑桑拉着绳子，将船拽到岸边，然后爬上船去，又去拉船那一头的绳子，不一会儿就到了对岸。桑桑上了岸，爬上大堤，这时，他看到了通往板仓的那条土路。他在大堤上的一棵大树下坐了下来，悄悄地等待着纸月走出板仓。

当太附升高了一截，大河上已无一丝雾气时，桑桑没有看到纸月，却看到土路上出现了三个男孩。他们在土路上晃

breath, just before the end of the first class. She raised her hand and said, "Here I am." The first few times, Jiang Yilun didn't take much notice. He just said, "Come in." But after a few more times, Jiang Yilun was a bit angry: "Zhi Yue, what's the matter? Why are you late everyday?"

Zhi Yue lowered her head.

"Be careful in the future. Go to your seat!" admonished Jiang Yilun.

Zhi Yue kept her head low. She sat down and still kept her head low.

By chance, Sang Sang glanced at Zhi Yue. He saw a string of tears falling down silently from her cheek onto her textbook.

One day, Sang Sang got up very early. He told his mother there was a pigeon missing last night. He was afraid it had been injured by an eagle. He had to look for it in the fields. He ran from home, hurrying toward Bancang. He wanted to find out what was happening to Zhi Yue.

When Sang Sang arrived at the riverside, the sun had just come out. The mist over the river was drifting away. There was a ferryboat on the river. There were ropes on each end of the ferryboat, fastening it to both banks. Sang Sang took the rope, pulled the boat to the bank, and climbed into it. He pulled the rope at the other end, and got to the opposite bank in no time. Sang Sang stepped out onto the bank, climbed up the embankment and saw the dirt path leading to Bancang. He sat down under a big tree on the embankment and waited for Zhi Yue quitely.

When the sun was higher and there was no mist left on the river, Sang Sang still didn't see Zhi Yue, but three boys

荡着，没有走开的意思，好像在等一个人。

桑桑不知道，这三个男孩都是板仓小学的学生。其中一个是板仓校园内有名的坏孩子，名叫刘一水，外号叫“豁嘴大茶壶”。其他两个是豁嘴大茶壶的“跟屁虫”，一个叫周德发，另一个叫吴天衡。桑桑更不知道，他们三个人是在等待纸月走过来。

过不一会儿，桑桑看到板仓村的村口，出现了纸月。

纸月迟迟疑疑地走过来了。她显然已经看到了刘一水。有一小会儿，纸月站在那儿不走了。但她看了看东边的太阳，还是走过来了。

刘一水直挺挺地横躺在路上，其他两个则坐在路边。

桑桑已经看出来了，他们要在这里欺负纸月。桑桑听父亲说过(父亲是听板仓小学的一位老师说的)，板仓小学有人专门爱欺负纸月，其中为首的一个叫豁嘴大茶壶。板仓小学曾几次想管束他们，但都没有什么效果，因为豁嘴大茶壶无法无天。桑桑想：这大概就是豁嘴大茶壶他们。桑桑才看到这儿，就已经明白纸月为什么总是天天迟到了。

纸月离刘一水们已经很近了。她又站了一会儿，然后跳进了路边的麦地。她要避开刘一水们。

刘一水们并不去追纸月，因为，在他们看来，纸月实际上是很难摆脱他们的。他们看见纸月在坑坑洼洼的麦地里走着，就咯咯咯地笑。笑了一阵，就一起扯着嗓子喊：

呀呀呀，呀呀呀，

脚趾缝里漏出一小丫。

were on the dirt path. They wandered on the path, as if waiting for someone.

Sang Sang didn't know the three boys were all Bancang Primary School pupils. One of them, Liu Yishui, nicknamed "harelip big kettle", was a well-known bad boy. The other two, Zhou Defa and Wu Tianheng, were his cohorts. Sang Sang also didn't know either, that they were waiting for Zhi Yue.

After a while, at the end of the village, Sang Sang saw Zhi Yue emerge.

Zhi Yue approached hesitantly. Apparently she had seen Liu Yishui. She stopped there. But she saw the sun in the east and finally resumed walking.

Liu Yishui lay flat on the road; the other two boys sat on the side of the road.

Now Sang Sang understood. They were here to bully Zhi Yue. He had heard from his father (who heard it from a teacher in Bancang Primary School) that boys were bullying Zhi Yue there, led by "harelip big kettle". The school tried to discipline them, but to no avail. "Harelip big kettle" was completely out of control. Sang Sang thought this must be the "harelip big kettle gang". Now it was clear why Zhi Yue was late every day.

Zhi Yue was already very close to Liu Yishui and the others. She stopped, and leaped into the wheat field to avoid the Liu Yishui gang.

The gang didn't chase Zhi Yue; they knew she couldn't get away from them. They saw Zhi Yue running in the bumpy field and jeered. They shouted out loud:

Ya Ya Ya, Ya Ya Ya,
A little girl dropped from between the toes,

没人搀，没人架，

刚一蹽腿就跌了个大趴叉。

这小丫，找不到家，

抹着眼泪胡哇哇……

他们一面叫，一面噼噼啪啪地拍着屁股伴奏。

纸月现在只惦记着赶紧上学，她不理会他们，斜穿麦地，往大堤上跑。

刘一水们眼见着纸月就要上大堤了，这才站起来也往大堤上跑去。

桑桑不能再在一旁看着了，他朝纸月大声叫道："纸月，往我这儿跑！往我这儿跑！"

纸月在麦地里站住了，望着大堤上的桑桑。

桑桑叫着："你快跑呀，你快跑呀！"

纸月这才朝大堤上跑过来。

在纸月朝大堤上跑过来时，桑桑一手抓了一块半截砖头，朝那边正跑过来的刘一水们走过去。

纸月爬上了大堤。

桑桑回头说了一声"你快点过河去"，继续走向刘一水们。

纸月站在那儿没有动。她呆呆地望着桑桑的背影，担忧而恐惧地等待着将要发生的斗殴。她想叫桑桑别再往前走了，但她没有叫。因为她知道桑桑是不肯回头的。

桑桑心里其实是害怕的。他不是板仓的人，他面对着的又是三个看上去都要比他大比他壮实的男孩。但桑桑很愿意当着纸月的面，好好地与人打一架。他在心里战栗地叫喊着：

Nobody supported or helped her,
She fell upside-down.
The little girl couldn't find home,
She wiped her tears and cried...

They shouted and slapped their buttocks to accompany the words.

Zhi Yue didn't take notice of them. She just wanted to go to school. She crossed the field and ran to the embankment.

The Liu Yishui gang saw Zhi Yue about to get to the embankment; they stood up and ran to the embankment too.

Sang Sang could no longer be a bystander. He shouted to Zhi Yue loudly, "Zhi Yue, come here, come here."

Zhi Yue stopped in the field and looked at Sang Sang on the embankment.

Sang Sang shouted, "Hurry up, hurry up!"

Zhi Yue came to herself and ran to the embankment.

While Zhi Yue ran, Sang Sang grabbed a piece of broken brick in each of his hands, and walked towards the gang.

Zhi Yue climbed down the embankment.

Sang Sang turned and told her, "You hurry and cross the river!" He kept on walking toward the gang.

Zhi Yue didn't move. She looked at the back of Sang Sang in a trance, worrying and fearful about the fighting to come. She wanted to ask Sang Sang not to go forward, but she didn't. She knew Sang Sang wouldn't retreat.

Sang Sang was frightened. He was not from Bancang and now he was facing three bigger, stronger boys. But Sang Sang wanted to put on a good fight in front of Zhi Yue. Trembling inside, he shouted, "Bring it on, bring it on!" His thin legs were

"你们来吧！你们来吧！"两条细腿却如寒风中的枝条，瑟瑟发抖。他甚至想先放下手中的砖头，到大树背后撒泡尿，因为他感觉到他的裤子已经有点潮湿了。

"桑桑……"纸月终于叫道。

桑桑没有回头，一手抓着一块半截砖头，站在那儿，等着刘一水他们过来。

刘一水先跑过来了，望着桑桑问："你是谁？"

"我是桑桑！"

"桑桑是什么东西？"刘一水说完，扭过头来朝周德发和吴天衡笑着。

桑桑把两块砖头抓得紧紧的，然后说："你们再往前走一步，我就砸了！"

刘一水说："你砸不准。"

桑桑说："我砸得准。"他吹起牛来："我想砸你的左眼，就绝不会砸到你的右眼上去。"但他随即觉得现在吹这个牛很可笑，就把腿叉开，摆出一副严阵以待的架势。

刘一水们互相搂着肩，根本就不把桑桑放在眼里，摆成一条线，大摇大摆地走过来了。桑桑举起了砖头，侧过身子，作出随时准备投掷的样子。刘一水们不知是因为害怕桑桑真的会用砖头砸中他们，还是因为被桑桑的那副凶样吓唬住了，暂时停了下来。

而这时，桑桑反而慢慢地往后退去。他在心里盘算着：当纸月登上渡船的一刹那间，他将砖头猛烈地投掷出去，然后也立即跳上渡船，将这一头的绳子解掉，赶紧将渡船拉向对岸。

shaking like branches in a cold wind. He wanted to put down his bricks and pee behind the big tree. He felt his trousers were a bit wet already.

"Sang Sang..." Zhi Yue finally shouted.

Sang Sang didn't turn his head. He held the bricks and stood there, waiting for the gang of Liu Yishui to come.

Liu Yishui came first. He demanded, "Who are you?"

"I am Sang Sang."

"Who the hell is that?" Liu Yishui said and turned to smile at Zhou Defa and Wu Tianheng.

Sang Sang clutched his two broken pieces of brick tightly and said, "I'll throw the bricks at you if you come one step further."

Liu Yishui said, "You can't hit us."

Sang Sang said, "Wait and see." He began to bluff: "If I want to hit your left eye, the brick won't hit your right eye." He immediately felt his bluffing was a bit funny. He planted his legs solidly apart and got ready for the fight.

The gang held each other's shoulders. They walked arrogantly in a row, not taking Sang Sang seriously at all.Sang Sang raised the brick, turned sideways and posed as if he were to throw at any time. The gang, perhaps fearful that Sang Sang might indeed hit them, or impressed with Sang Sang's fierce appearance, stopped.

Sang Sang, on the contrary, retreated slowly. He was thinking that at the moment Zhi Yue climbed onto the ferryboat, he would throw the bricks really hard, then immediately jump onto the boat, untie the rope on one end, and quickly pull the boat to the other bank.

纸月似乎明白了桑桑的意图，就往大堤下跑，直奔渡船。

桑桑就这么抓着砖头，一边瞪着刘一水们，一边往后退着。刘一水们还真的不敢轻举妄动，只是在一定的距离内，一步一步地逼过来。

桑桑掉头看了一眼。当看到纸月马上就要跑到水边时，他突然朝前冲去，吓得刘一水们掉头往后逃窜。而桑桑却在冲出去几步之后，掉头往大堤下冲去。桑桑一边冲，一边很为他的这一点点狡猾得意。

刘一水们终于站住，转身反扑过来。

桑桑朝纸月大声叫着："快上船！快上船！"

纸月连忙上了船。

桑桑已退到水边。当他看到刘一水们已追到跟前时，心里说："我不怕砸破了你们的头！"然后猛地将一块砖头投掷出去。然而用力过猛，那砖头竟落到刘一水们身后去了。不过倒也把刘一水们吓了一跳。这时，桑桑趁机跳上了船。刘一水们正要去抓拴在大树上的绳子，桑桑就又将手中的另一块砖头也投掷了出去。这回砸到了吴天衡的脚上，疼得他瘫在地上"哎哟哎哟"地叫唤。但就在桑桑要去解绳子时，刘一水却已抓住了绳子，把正被纸月拉向对岸的船，又拉了回去。绳子系得太死，桑桑费了很大的劲，才将它解开，而这时，船已几乎靠岸了。刘一水飞跑过来，不顾桑桑的阻拦，一步跳到了船上。

纸月用力地将船向对岸拉去。

刘一水朝纸月扑过来，想从纸月手里抢过绳子。

Zhi Yue seemed to realize what was on Sang Sang's mind. She ran down the embankment to the boat.

Sang Sang clutched the bricks, stared at the gang and retreated. The gang wasn't sure what to do. They moved towards Sang Sang but kept their distance.

Sang Sang turned and glanced back. When he saw that Zhi Yue was near the riverside, he suddenly charged forward, scaring the gang off. After a few steps, Sang Sang turned back and rushed down the embankment. He was really proud of his trick.

The gang finally stopped, turned and ran after him.

Sang Sang shouted loudly to Zhi Yue, "Hurry up - to the boat!"

Zhi Yue scrambled into the boat.

Sang Sang retreated to the riverside. When he saw the gang near him, he thought, "I don't care if I hit you!" He threw a brick hard towards them. He used so much force that the brick fell behind the gang. But it did frighten them. Sang Sang grabbed the opportunity and jumped into the boat. The gang tried to grab the rope tied to the tree. Sang Sang threw another brick at them. This time it landed on Wu Tianheng's foot. He was in great pain and sank on the ground and screamed. When Sang Sang tried to untie the rope, Liu Yishui grabbed it. The boat, being pulled to the other bank by Zhi Yue, came back. Sang Sang made an enormous effort to untie the knot, but it was too tight. The boat was almost ashore. Liu Yishui ran over to the boat, repelled Sang Sang, and jumped in.

Zhi Yue tried hard to pull the boat to the other bank.

Liu Yishui ran to Zhi Yue, trying to pull the rope from her hands.

桑桑双手抱住了刘一水的腰，两人在船舱里打了起来。桑桑根本不是刘一水的对手，勉强纠缠了一阵，就被刘一水打翻在船舱，骑在了胯下。刘一水擦了一把汗，望着桑桑："从哪儿冒出来个桑桑！"说完，就给了桑桑一拳。

桑桑觉得自己的鼻梁一阵锐利的酸疼，随即，鼻孔就流出血来。

桑桑看到了一个野蛮的面孔。他想给刘一水重重一击，但他根本无法动弹。

刘一水又给了桑桑几拳。

纸月放下了绳子，哭着："你别再打他了，你别再打他了……"

刘一水眼看渡船已离岸很远，就将桑桑扔下了，然后跑到船头上，趴下来卷起袖子，用手将船往回划着。

桑桑躺在舱底一动也不动地仰望着冬天的天空。他从未在这样一个奇特的角度看过天空。在这样的角度所看到的天空，显得格外的高阔。他想，如果这时，他的鸽子在天空飞翔，一定会非常好看的。河上有风，船在晃动，桑桑的天空也在晃动。桑桑有一种说不出来的晕眩感。

纸月坐在船头上，任刘一水将船往回划。

桑桑看到了一朵急急飘去的白云，这朵白云使桑桑忽然有些紧张。他慢慢爬起来，然后朝刘一水爬过去。当渡船离

Sang Sang held Liu Yishui's wrist with both hands. The two began fighting in the boat, but Sang Sang wasn't a match for Liu Yishui. He fought for a while before falling backward to the deck, then Liu Yishui sat on him. Liu Yishui wiped his sweat off and stared at Sang Sang. "Where in hell did you come from!" He punched Sang Sang hard.

Sang Sang felt a fierce pain on his nose. Next, he felt blood dripping down.

Sang Sang was looking up at a barbaric face. He wanted to strike Liu Yishui but he couldn't move.

Liu Yishui struck him again.

Zhi Yue put down the rope and cried, "Don't hit him, don't hit him..."

Liu Yishui saw that the boat was far away from the bank. He let go of Sang Sang, ran to the front of the boat, lay down, rolled up his sleeves and started to paddle the boat back with his hands.

Sang Sang lay on the floor of the boat, motionless, staring at the winter sky. He had never seen the sky from such a strange angle. The sky was incredibly high and wide from this perspective. He thought, if his pigeons flew past, it would make such a pretty scene. There was wind over the river, the boat was shaking, and the sky in Sang Sang's vision was shaking too. He felt an indescribable dizziness.

Zhi Yue sat in the front of the boat, letting Liu Yishui paddle the boat back.

Sang Sang saw a piece of cloud hurrying off, which made him nervous. He got up slowly and climbed over to Liu Yishui. When the boat was a dozen meters away from the bank, Sang

岸还有十几米远时，桑桑突然一头撞过去。随即，他和纸月都听到了扑通一声。他趴在船帮上，兴奋地看着一团水花。过不一会儿，刘一水挣扎出水面。桑桑站起来，用手擦着鼻孔下的两道血流，俯视着在冬天的河水中艰难游动着的刘一水。

纸月将船朝对岸拉去。

当刘一水游回岸边，因为寒冷而哆哆嗦嗦地跳动时，桑桑和纸月也已站在了河这边柔软的草地上。

6

刘一水跑回家换了衣裳，快近中午时，就觉得浑身发冷，乌了的嘴唇直打颤。放学后，他勉强回到家中，就着凉生病了。刘一水的家长闹到了油麻地小学，闹到了桑乔家。这么一闹，就把事情闹大了，事情一闹大，事情也就好收拾了。到处都有桑乔的学生。桑乔赔了礼之后，联合了板仓小学，甚至联合了地方政府，一起出面，将刘一水等几个孩子连同他们的家长找到一起，发出严重警告：假如日后再有一丝欺负纸月的行为，学校与地方政府都将对刘一水等人以及他们的家长进行老实不客气的处理。

这天，桑乔对纸月说："纸月，板仓那边，已没有人再敢欺负你了，你还是回那边读书吧。"

纸月低着头，不吭声。

Sang suddenly slammed into him. Zhi Yue and he immediately saw and heard a big splash. He leaned against the edge of the boat, looking excitedly at the spray, as Liu Yishui struggled to get to the bank. Sang Sang stood up, wiping off the blood under his nose with his hand, and watching Liu Yishui thrashing about in the freezing river of winter.

Zhi Yue pulled the boat to the opposite bank.

By the time Liu Yishui had swam to the bank, shaking and jumping from the cold, Sang Sang and Zhi Yue were standing on the soft grass on the opposite side.

6

Liu Yishui ran home and changed his clothes. He felt cold all over at noon, his blue lips trembling. After school, he managed to walk home and immediately fell ill. His family stirred things up at Youmadi Primary School and at Sang Qiao's home. The incident suddenly became a big event; now, it became easier to deal with. Sang Qiao had students everywhere. He apologized to the family. But after that, he joined with the Bancang Primary School and even the local government, to summon the gang of Liu Yishui and their families and gave them a stern warning. If they were to bully Zhi Yue again, the school and the local government would not fail to punish the gang and their families.

Sang Qiao told Zhi Yue, "Zhi Yue, nobody dares to bully you in the future. You'd better go back to study there."

Zhi Yue held her head low and didn't speak.

“你跟你外婆好好商量一下。”

纸月点点头，回教室去了。

桑桑的母亲说：“就让她在这儿念书吧。”

桑乔说：“这没有问题，就怕这孩子跑坏了身体。”

那一天，纸月坐在课堂上，没有一点儿心思听课，目光空空的。

第二天一早，纸月和外婆就出现在桑桑家门口。

外婆对桑乔说：“她只想在油麻地读书。你就再收留她吧。”

桑乔望着纸月：“你想好了?”

纸月不说话，只是点点头。

在一旁喂鸽子的桑桑，就一直静静地听着。等外婆与纸月走后，他将他的鸽子全都轰上了天空，鸽子飞得高兴时，噼噼啪啪地击打双翅，仿佛满空里都响着一片清脆的掌声。

一切，一如往常。

但不久，桑桑感觉到有几个孩子在用异样的目光看他，看纸月。并且，他们越来越放肆了。比如，上体育课，当他正好与纸月分在一个小组时，以朱小鼓为首的那几个人，就会莫名其妙地“嗷”地叫一声。羞愤的桑桑，揪住一个孩子的衣领，把他拖到屋后的竹林里给了一拳。但桑桑的反应，更刺激了朱小鼓们。他们并无恶意，但一个个都觉得这种哄闹实在太来劲了。他们中间甚至有桑桑最要好的朋友。

"You go and talk with your grandmother."

Zhi Yue nodded and went back to the classroom.

Sang Sang's mother said, "Let her study here."

Sang Qiao said, "It is fine with me. But it is such a distance that I worry about her health."

Zhi Yue sat in the classroom. She wasn't concentrating at all; her eyes were empty.

Early next morning, Zhi Yue and her grandmother appeared at the door of Sang Sang's.

The grandmother said to Sang Qiao, "She just wants to study at Youmadi. Please do take her."

Sang Qiao looked at Zhi Yue, "Have you made up your mind?"

Zhi Yue didn't speak, just nodded.

Sang Sang was feeding the pigeons at the side of the house. He was listening quietly. When Zhi Yue and her grandmother left, he shooed away all his pigeons. When they were happy, the pigeons flapped their wings hard, and the sky seemed to be full of resounding applause.

Things went back to normal.

Shortly after the incident, Sang Sang felt there were a few kids looking at him and Zhi Yue strangely. And they became more and more rude. In the physical exercises class, if Sang Sang happened to be in the same group as Zhi Yue, they would make funny noises, led by Zhu Xiaogu. Embarassed and furious, Sang Sang grabbed the collar of one of them, dragged him to the bamboo grove behind the classroom and hit him. But Sang Sang's reaction further incited Zhu Xiaogu and the others. They didn't mean wrong -- they just felt it was really exciting fun. Among them were even Sang Sang's best friends.

桑桑这种孩子，从小就注定了要成为别人哄闹的对象。

这天下午是作文课。桑桑的作文一直是被蒋一轮夸奖的。而上一回做的一篇作文，尤其做得好，整篇文章差不多全被蒋一轮圈点了。这堂作文课的第一个节目就是让桑桑朗读他的作文。这是事先说好了的。上课铃一响，蒋一轮走上讲台，说："今天，我们请桑桑同学朗读他的作文《我们去麦地里》。"

但桑桑却在满头大汗地翻书包：他的作文本不见了。

蒋一轮说："别着急，慢慢找。"

慢慢找也找不到。桑桑失望了，站在那儿抓耳挠腮。

蒋一轮朝桑桑咂了一下嘴，问道："谁看到桑桑的作文本了？"

大家就立即去看自己的桌肚，翻自己的书包。不一会儿，就陆续有人说："我这儿没有。"

而当纸月将书包里的东西都取出来查看时，脸一下子红了：在她的作文本下，压着桑桑的作文本。

有一两个孩子一眼看到了桑桑的作文本，就把目光停在了纸月的脸上。

纸月只好将桑桑的作文本从她的作文本下抽出，然后站起来："报告，桑桑的作文本在我这儿。"她拿着作文本，朝讲台上走去。

朱小鼓领头，"嗷"地叫了一声。随即，几乎是全教室的孩子，都跟着"嗷"起来。

蒋一轮用黑板擦一拍讲台："安静！"

蒋一轮接过纸月手中的桑桑的作文本，然后又送到桑桑手上。

Sang Sang was a boy to be made fun of by others.

It was writing class one afternoon. Sang Sang's compositions were often praised by Jiang Yilun. His last one was especially good. Jiang Yilun marked many red circles on it in approbation. The first item in this writing class was to have Sang Sang read his composition; it had been scheduled in advance. When the bell rang, Jiang Yilun walked to the teaching stand and said, "Today, let's ask Sang Sang to read his composition '*We are going to the wheat fields.*'"

Sang Sang searched in his bag, sweating. His compositions exercise book was missing.

Jiang Yilun said, "Take it easy; you can find it."

He took it easy but still couldn't find it. Sang Sang was disappointed, scratching his ears and cheeks.

Jiang Yilun looked inquiringly at Sang Sang and asked, "Who has seen Sang Sang's compositions exercise book?"

Students all searched in their desks and bags. After a while, they said one by one, "I don't have it."

When Zhi Yue took everything out of her bag, she turned red. Sang Sang's compositions exercise book was under hers.

A couple of students saw it and stared at Zhi Yue.

Zhi Yue took Sang Sang's compositions exercise book from under hers and stood up: "It's here." She took the exercise book and walked to the teacher's stand.

Zhu Xiaogu led the shouting. Immediately, all the kids followed.

Jiang Yilun struck the teacher's desk with a brush. "Silence!"

He took the exercise book from Zhi Yue and passed it to Sang Sang.

桑桑开始读他自己的作文，但读得结结巴巴，仿佛那作文不是他写的，而是抄别人的。

写得蛮好的一篇作文，经桑桑这么吭哧吭哧地一读，谁也觉不出好来，课堂秩序乱糟糟的。蒋一轮皱着眉头，硬是坚持着听桑桑把他的作文读完。

放学后，朱小鼓看到了桑桑，朝他诡秘地一笑。

桑桑不理他，蹲了下来，装着系鞋带，眼睛却瞟着朱小鼓。当看到朱小鼓走到池塘边上打算撅下一根树枝抓在手中玩耍时，他突然站起来冲了过去，双手一推，将朱小鼓推了下去。这池塘刚出了藕，水倒是没有，但全是稀泥。朱小鼓是一头栽下去的。等他将脑袋从烂泥里拔出来时，除了两只眼睛闪闪发亮，其余地方，全都被烂泥糊住了。他恼了，顺手抓了两把烂泥爬了上来。

桑桑没有逃跑。

朱小鼓跑过来，把两把烂泥都砸在了桑桑的身上。

桑桑放下书包，一纵身跳进烂泥塘，也抓了两把烂泥，就在塘里，直接把烂泥砸到了朱小鼓身上。

朱小鼓抹了一把脸上的泥，也跳进烂泥塘里。

孩子们闪在一边，无比兴奋地看着这场泥糊大战。

纸月站在教室里，从门缝里悄悄向外看着。

不一会儿工夫，桑桑与朱小鼓身上就再也找不出一块干净地方了。老师们看着这两个“泥猴”，一边大声制止着，却又一边抑制不住地笑着。

Sang Sang began to read his composition. But he stammered, as if he had not written the article.

It was a good article, but by the erratic way Sang Sang read it, no one could appreciate it. The classroom was a bit uneasy. Jiang Yilun knitted his brows, and waited patiently for Sang Sang to finish reading.

After school, Zhu Xiaogu saw Sang Sang and threw a bizarre smile at him.

Sang Sang ignored him. He squatted and pretended to tie his shoelaces. He glanced at Zhu Xiaogu. When Zhu Xiaogu walked to the side of the pond, tried to pick a branch and play with it, Sang Sang suddenly charged and pushed Zhu Xiaogu into the pond. Only lotus grew in the pond; there was no water, just mud. Zhu Xiaogu fell into it headfirst. When he raised his head out of the mud, his whole body was covered, except for his shining eyes. He was furious; he grabbed some mud and climbed up and out of the pond.

Sang Sang didn't run.

Zhu Xiaogu ran over and hit Sang Sang with the mud.

Sang Sang put down his bag, jumped into the mud pond, took more mud, and hit Zhu Xiaogu with it.

Zhu Xiaogu wiped the mud off his face, and jumped into the mud pond too.

Children gathered, excitedly watching the mud fight.

Zhi Yue stood in the classroom, stealing a look from the small opening of the door.

After a while, there was not a single clean spot on the bodies of either boys. Teachers saw the two "muddy monkeys" and shouted at them to stop, while convulsed with laughter.

孩子们无所谓站在哪一边，只是不住地拍着巴掌。

蒋一轮终于板下脸来："桑桑，朱小鼓，你们立即给我停住!"

两人也没有什么力气了，勉强又互相砸了几把烂泥，就弯下腰去，在烂泥塘里到处找自己的鞋袜。孩子们就过来看，并指着烂泥塘的某一个位置叫道："在那边!在那边!"

桑桑爬上来时，偶然朝教室看了一眼。他看到了藏在门后的纸月的眼睛。

两天后，天下起了入冬以来最大的一场雪。

教室后面的竹林深处，躲避风雪的一群麻雀唧唧喳喳地叫着，闹得孩子们都听不清老师讲课。仅仅是一堂课的时间，再打开教室门时，门口就已堆积了足有一尺深的雪。到了傍晚放学时，一块一块的麦地都已被大雪厚厚覆盖，田埂消失了，眼前只是一个平坦无边的大雪原。然而，大雪还在稠密生猛地下着。

孩子们艰难地走出了校园，然后像一颗颗黑点，散落在雪野上。

桑桑的母亲站在院门口，等纸月。中午，她就与纸月说好了，让她今天不要回家，放了学就直接来这儿。当她看到校园里已剩下不多的孩子时，便朝教室走来。路上遇到了桑桑，她问："纸月呢?"

桑桑指着很远处的一个似有似无的黑点："她回家了。"

Children didn't take sides; they just kept on applauding.

Jiang Yilun finally put on a stern face. "Sang Sang, Zhu Xiaogu, stop now!"

They were both exhausted, but still managed to hit each other a bit more. Then they bent down to look for their shoes and socks in the mud pond. Children came over and pointed: "Over there, over there!"

Sang Sang climbed out and glanced at the classroom. He saw the eyes of Zhi Yue hiding at the door.

Two days later came the biggest snow of the winter.

A flock of sparrows hid in the depth of the bamboo grove behind the classroom, finding shelter from the snow and wind. They were so noisy that students could hardly hear the lecture. When the door was opened, it was seen that in the time of only one class, one chi' of snow had fallen. By dusk, when school was over, the wheat fields were covered by thick snow. The low banks of earth between the fields were gone. What was ahead was a limitless snow plain. The heavy snow still continued to fall.

Children struggled to walk out of the schoolyard, scattering on the snow plain like black spots.

Sang Sang's mother stood at the entrance of the courtyard waiting for Zhi Yue. At midday, she had told Zhi Yue not to go home, but to wait for her after school. There were not many students left on the campus, so Sang Sang's mother came to the classroom. She met Sang Sang on her way and asked, "Where is Zhi Yue?"

Sang Sang pointed to a half-visible black spot in the distance. "She went home."

“你没有留她?”

桑桑站在那儿不动,朝大雪中那个向前慢慢移动的黑点看着——整个雪野上，就那么一个黑点。

桑桑的母亲在桑桑的后脑勺上打了一巴掌：“你八成是欺负她了。”

桑桑突然哭起来:“我没有欺负她，我没有欺负她……”扭头往家走去。

桑桑的母亲跟着桑桑走进院子：“你没有欺负她，她怎么走了?”

桑桑一边抹眼泪，一边跺着脚，向母亲大叫：“我没有欺负她!我没有欺负她!我哪儿欺负她了?!”

他抓了两团雪，将它们攥结实，然后，直奔鸽笼，狠狠地向那些正缩着脖子歇在屋檐下的鸽子砸去。

鸽子们被突如其来的攻击惊呆了，愣了一下，随即慌张地飞起。有几只钻进笼里的，将脑袋伸出来看了看，没有立即起飞。桑桑一见，又攥了两个雪球砸过去，鸽笼咚的一声巨响，惊得最后几只企图不飞的鸽子，也只好飞进风雪里。

鸽子们在天空中吃力地飞着。它们不肯远飞，就在草房子的上空盘旋，总有要立即落下来的心思。

桑桑却见着什么抓什么，只顾往空中乱砸乱抡，绝不让它们落下。

"You didn't stop her?"

Sang Sang stood there motionless, looking at the slow-moving black spot in the heavy snow. There was only one black spot in the whole snow plain now.

Sang Sang's mother hit him on the back of his head, "You must have bullied her."

Sang Sang burst into tears, "No, I didn't, I didn't..." He turned and walked towards home.

His mother followed him to the courtyard, "If you didn't bully her, why did she leave?"

Sang Sang wiped his tears, stamped his feet, and roared at his mother, "I didn't bully her! I didn't bully her! How could I bully her?!"

He took some snow, kneaded it tight into two balls, ran straight to the pigeon's cage, and hit the pigeons hard. The pigeons had pulled in their necks and were resting under the eaves.

The pigeons were startled by the unexpected attack. They were stupefied for a moment before quickly taking off. A few had been in the cage; they now poked their heads out to see what was happening, and didn't fly away immediately. Sang Sang saw them, formed two more snowballs and hit them. There was a heavy sound, and the remaining few pigeons took off into the wind and snow.

They struggled in the sky. They couldn't fly far. So they just circled above in the sky, ready to fly down to land any time.

Sang Sang grabbed anything he saw and threw them into the sky, determined not to allow the pigeons down.

鸽子们见这儿实在落不下来，就落到了其他草房顶上。这使桑桑更恼火。他立即跑出院子，追着砸那些企图落在其他草房顶上的鸽子。

母亲看着跑得上气不接下气的桑桑：“你疯啦？”

桑桑头一歪：“我没有欺负她！我没有欺负她嘛！”说着，用手背猛地抹了一把眼泪。

“那你就砸鸽子？”

“我愿意砸！我愿意砸！”他操起一根竹竿，使劲地朝空中飞翔的鸽子挥舞不止，嘴里却在不住地说，“我没有欺负她嘛！我没有欺负她嘛……”

鸽子们终于知道，它们在短时间内，在草房子上是落不下来了，只好冒着风雪朝远处飞去。

桑桑站在那儿，看着它们渐渐远去，与雪混成一色，直到再也无法区别。

桑桑再往前看，朦胧的泪眼里，那个黑点已完全消失在黄昏时分的风雪里。

The pigeons saw that they could not land there, so they flew to the rooftops of other straw houses. This irritated Sang Sang even more. He immediately ran out of the courtyard, chasing after the pigeons as they tried to land.

His mother saw him, out of breath, and asked, "Are you mad?"

Sang Sang tilted his head back: "I didn't bully her. I didn't bully her!" He wiped his tears abruptly with the back of his hand.

"So you hit the pigeons?"

"Yes, I just want to hit them!" He took a bamboo pole, waved it hard at the pigeons flying in the sky. He wouldn't stop shouting "I didn't bully her! I didn't bully her..."

The pigeons realized finally there was no way they could descend to the straw houses for a while. They had to fly away against the wind and snow.

Sang Sang stood there, and saw them slowly flying away. They merged with the snow and became invisible.

Sang Sang looked further. In his misty eyes, the black spot had completely disappeared in the wind and snow of the dusk.

细马

1

与桑桑家关系最密切的人家，是邱元龙邱二爷家。

邱二爷家独自住在一处，离桑桑家倒不算很远。

邱家早先开牙行，也是个家底厚实的人家。后来牙行不开了，但邱二爷仍然做掮客，到集市上介绍牛的买卖。姓王的要买姓李的牛，买的一方吃不准那条牛的脾性，不知道那牛有无暗病，这时就需要有一个懂行的中间人作保；而卖的一方，总想卖出一个好价钱，需要一个懂行的中间人来帮助他点明他家这条牛的种种好处，让对方识货。邱二爷这个人很可靠。他看牛，也就是看牛，绝不动手看牙口，或拍胯骨，看了，就知道这条牛在什么样的档次上。卖的，买的，只要是邱二爷做介绍人，就都觉得这买卖公平。邱二爷人又厚道，不像一些掮客为一己利益而尽靠嘴皮子去鼓动人卖，或鼓动人买。他只说：“你花这么多钱买这头牛，合适。”或说：“你的这条牛卖这么多钱，合适。”卖的，买的，都知道邱二爷对他们负责。因此，邱二爷的生意很好，拿的佣金也多。

Xi Ma

I

The family closest to the Sangs were the Qius. Qiu Yunlong was the second among his siblings, called Old Qiu 2nd.

The Qius lived in a detached house not far away from the Sang's.

Originally, the Qius ran a dentist's, and were rather prosperous. Later they no longer ran the store but Old Qiu 2nd was still a cattle broker in the market. If Wang wanted to buy Li's cattle, but was unsure of the cattle's temperament or possible hidden sickness, he would need a professional broker to act as a guarantor. The seller wanted to get a good price; he too needed a professional broker to point out good things about his cattle, so that the buyer could appreciate their qualities. Old Qiu 2nd was very reliable. When he looked at the cattle, he never touched them it to see their teeth or patted their hipbones. He could appraise the animal by merely looking at it. When Old Qiu 2nd was the broker, the seller and the buyer knew they could get a fair deal. He was an honest man; he would never try to talk or push anyone into selling or buying. He just said "It is alright to spend this amount of money to buy the cattle", or "It is fine to sell your cattle at this price." Both seller and the buyer knew Old Qiu 2nd was responsible to them. For this reason, he had good business and a lot of commissions.

邱二妈是油麻地有名的俏二妈。油麻地的人们都说，邱二妈嫁到油麻地时，是当时最美的女子。邱二妈现在虽然是五十多岁的人了，但依旧很有光彩。邱二妈一年四季总是一尘不染的样子。邱二妈的头发天天都梳得很认真，搽了油，太阳一照，发亮。发髻盘得很讲究，仿佛是盘了几天才盘成的。髻上套了黑网，插一根镶了玉的簪子。那玉很润，很亮。

邱二爷与邱二妈建了一个很好的家：好房子、好庭院、好家什。

但这个家有一个极大的缺憾：没有孩子。

这个缺憾对于邱二爷与邱二妈来说，是刻骨铭心的。他们该做的都做了，但最终还是未能有一个孩子。当他们终于不再抱希望时，就常常会在半夜里醒来，然后，就在一种寂寞里，一种对未来茫然无底的恐慌里，一种与人丁兴旺的人家相比之后而感到的自卑里，凄凄惶惶地等到天亮。望着好房子、好庭院、好家什，他们更感到这一切实在没有多大意思。

当初，邱二妈在想孩子而没有孩子，再见到别人家的孩子时，竟克制不住地表示她的喜欢。她总是把这些孩子叫回家中，给他们花生吃或红枣、柿饼吃。如果是还在母亲怀抱中的孩子，她就会对那孩子的母亲说："让我抱抱。"抱了，就不怎么肯放下来。但到了终于明白绝对不可能再有孩子时，她忽然对孩子淡漠了。她嫌孩子太闹，嫌孩子弄乱了她屋子

His wife Madam Qiu 2nd was well-known in Youmadi for her good looks. Local people said that she was the most beautiful lady of the area when she came to Youmadi to get married. Now she was over fifty, but still pretty. She was always spotless, all year around. She combed her hair neatly everyday and applied oil to it -- it glittered under the sun. Her chignon was carefully coiled, as if she had spent days doing it. A black net covered her chignon, with a jade hairpin in it. The jade was very smooth and glossy.

The couple built a nice house -- attractive rooms, a nice courtyard and good furniture.

But there was a great piece missing in the family -- the couple had no children.

It was heart-wrenching pain for the couple. They did everything they could, but their wish was still not satisfied. Finally they gave up. Often they woke up in the middle of the night, sunk in solitude and a bottomless fear for the future, thinking of those families with many children, and waited sadly and wretchedly for the daylight. They did have nice rooms, courtyard and furniture, but what was the point?

Initially, Madam Qiu 2nd wanted kids badly, and when she saw other people's children, she couldn't help showing her affection for them. She always took kids home, giving them peanuts, dates and persimmon cakes. For those infants still in their mothers' embrace, she would say to the mothers, "Let me hold your baby." And she wouldn't let it go. Finally when she realized there was no way she could have a child, she suddenly became cold to children. She disliked children's noise, and their making a mess of her household. Parents

里的东西。因此，有孩子的人家就提醒自己的孩子：“别去邱二妈家。邱二妈不喜欢孩子进她家里。”

当他们忽然在一天早上感到自己已经老了，而身边必须有一个年轻的生命时，他们预感到一种悲哀正在向他们一步一步地走来。他们几乎已经望见了一个凄凉的老年。

他们想起了生活在江南一个小镇上的邱二爷的大哥：他竟有四个儿子。

于是，邱二爷带着他与邱二妈商量了几夜之后而确定的一个意图——从邱大家过继来一个儿子——出发了。

仅隔十天，邱二爷就回到了油麻地。他带回了本章的主人公，一个叫细马的男孩。

这是邱大最小的儿子，一个长得很精神的男孩，大额头双眼微眍，眼珠微黄，但亮得出奇，两颗门牙略大，预示着长大了，是一个有大力气的男人。

然而，邱二妈在见到细马之后仅仅十分钟，就忽然从单纯地观看一个男孩的喜欢里走了出来，换了一副冷冰冰的脸色。

邱二爷知道邱二妈为什么抖落出这副脸色。他在邱二妈走出屋子、走进厨房后不久，也走进了厨房里。

邱二妈在刷锅，不吭声。

邱二爷说：“老大只同意我把最小的这一个带回来。”

邱二妈把舀水的瓢扔到了水缸里：“等把他养大了，我们的骨头早变成灰了。”

邱二爷坐在凳子上，双手抱着头。

reminded their kids, "Don't go to the Qius. Madam Qiu 2nd doesn't like children in her house."

One morning, the couple suddenly realized they were getting old, and they desperately wanted a young person around. They felt a looming sorrow approaching them ever-closer. They could almost see their miserable old age.

They thought of Old Qiu 2nd's elder brother living in a small town in the region south of the Yangtze River. He had four sons!

The couple discussed it for nights and came to a conclusion -- they could adopt a son from Old Qiu 1st. Old Qiu 2nd set out.

Only ten days later, Old Qiu 2nd came back to Youmadi with the main character of this chapter -- a boy named Xi Ma.

Xi Ma was the smallest son of Old Qiu 1st. He looked energetic, with a big forehead and a pair of slightly sunken eyes. His eyeballs were a bit yellowish but extremely shiny. His two front teeth were rather big, indicating that he would be a strong man when he grew up.

However, merely ten minutes after Madam Qiu 2nd saw Xi Ma, she turned abruptly from happiness to cold.

Old Qiu 2nd knew why his wife acted like this. He followed her out of the room and to the kitchen.

Madam Qiu 2nd was wordlessly washing a pot.

Old Qiu 2nd said, "My brother would let me take only his youngest son."

Madam Qiu 2nd threw the gourd ladle into the water tank, "When he grows up, we will have become ashes."

Old Qiu 2nd sat on a stool, holding his head with both hands.

邱二妈说："他倒会盘算。大的留着，大的有用了。把小的给了人，小的还得花钱养活他。我们把他养大，然后再把这份家产都留给他。我们又图个什么？你大哥也真会拿主意！"

"那怎么办？人都已被我领回来了。"

"让他玩几天，把他再送回去。"

"说得容易，我把他的户口都迁出来了，在我口袋里呢。"

邱二妈刷着锅，刷着刷着就哭了。

这时细马站在厨房门口，操一口邱二爷和邱二妈都不太听得懂的江南口音问："院子里是一棵什么树？"

邱二爷去看邱大，到过江南好几回，勉强听得懂江南话，说："乌桕。"

"上面是一个鸟窝吗？"

"是个鸟窝。"

"什么鸟的窝？"

"喜鹊。"

"树上没有喜鹊。"

"它们飞出去了。"

细马就仰头望天空。天空没有喜鹊，只有鸽子。他一边望，一边问："谁家的鸽子？"

"桑桑家的。"

"桑桑是个大人吗？"

"跟你差不多大。"

Madam Qiu 2nd said, "Your brother is really cunning. He keeps his elder sons who can work now. He gives away the small one for others to feed. We bring up his youngest son and leave our fortune to him. What's in it for us? Your brother is so calculating!"

"What can we do now? I have taken the boy."

"Let him have fun for a few days. Then we will send him back."

"It won't be that easy. I have transferred his registration. The paper is in my pocket."

Madam Qiu 2nd was scrubbing the pot, and she cried.

Xi Ma stood at the door of the kitchen. In his southern dialect which Old Qiu 2nd and his wife didn't understand very well, he asked, "What's the tree in the courtyard called?"

Old Qiu 2nd had been to the region south of the Yangtze River a few times to see his brother, so he understood a bit of the southern dialect. He answered, "It's a Chinese tallow tree."

"Is that a bird's nest on the top?"

"Yes it is."

"What bird?"

"Magpie."

"There are no magpies in the tree."

"They have flown away."

Xi Ma raised his head to look at the sky. There were no magpies in the sky, just pigeons. He asked, "Whose pigeons are those?"

"Sang Sang's."

"Is Sang Sang a grownup?"

"He is about your age."

“他家远吗？”

“前面有座桥，在桥那边。”

“我去找他玩。”

邱二爷刚要阻止，细马已经跑出院子。

桑桑见到了细马。起初细马很有说话的欲望，但当他发现他的话很难让桑桑听得懂之后，就不吭声了，很陌生地站在一旁看着桑桑喂鸽子。

细马走后，桑桑对母亲说：“他是一个江南小蛮子。”

邱二爷领着细马来找桑乔，说细马转学的事。桑乔问：“读几年级？”

邱二爷说：“该读四年级了，跟桑桑一样。”

桑乔说：“你去找蒋一轮老师，就说我同意了。”

蒋一轮要摸底，出了几张卷子让细马做。卷子放在蒋一轮的办公桌上，细马坐在蒋一轮坐的椅子上，瞪着眼睛把卷子看了半天，才开始答。答一阵，又停住了，挖一挖鼻孔，或摸一摸耳朵，一副很无奈的样子。蒋一轮收了卷子，看了看，对桑乔说：“细马最多只能读三年级。”

邱二妈来到桑桑家，对桑乔说：“还是让他读四年级吧。”

桑乔说：“怕跟不上。”

"Does he live far away?"

"There is a bridge ahead. He lives on the other side of the bridge."

"I'm going to look for him."

Old Qiu 2nd wanted to stop him, but Xi Ma had run out of the courtyard.

Sang Sang saw Xi Ma. Initially Xi Ma was eager to talk. But when he found Sang Sang could hardly understand him, he went silent. He saw Sang Sang feeding the pigeons; he waited on the side, feeling like a stranger.

After Xi Ma went away, Sang Sang told his mother, "He is a little southern barbarian."

Old Qiu 2nd took Xi Ma to see Sang Qiao and discussed transferring Xi Ma to the school. Sang Qiao asked, "Which grade is he in?"

He said, "He should be in grade four, like Sang Sang."

Sang Qiao said, "Go look for teacher Jiang. Tell him I agreed to it."

Jiang Yilun wanted to see how Xi Ma was doing in his studies, so he asked him to do a few examination papers. Xi Ma sat on Jiang Yilun's chair to do the papers on Jiang Yilun's desk. He stared at the papers for a long time before starting. After a while, he paused, digging his nose or scratching his ears, looking helpless. Jiang Yilun took the papers, had a glimpse and told Sang Qiao, "He could manage grade three at best."

Madam Qiu 2nd came to Sang Sang's home and said to Sang Qiao, "Let Xi Ma study in grade four."

Sang Qiao said, "I'm afraid he might not be able to catch up."

邱二妈说："我看他也不是个读书的料，就这么跟着混混拉倒了。"

桑乔苦笑了一下："我再跟蒋老师说说。"

细马就成了桑桑的同学。

细马被蒋一轮带到班上时，孩子们都用一种新鲜但又怪异的目光去看他。因为他是从遥远的地方来的一个小蛮子。

细马和秃鹤合用一张课桌。

细马看了看秃鹤的头，笑了，露出几颗大门牙。

秃鹤低声道："小蛮子！"

细马听不懂，望望他，望望你，意思是说：这个秃子在说什么？

孩子们就笑了起来。

细马不知道孩子们在笑什么，觉得自己似乎也该跟着笑，就和孩子们一起笑。

孩子们便大笑。

秃鹤又说了一句："小蛮子！"

细马依然不知道秃鹤在说什么。

孩子们就一起小声叫了起来："小蛮子！"

细马不知为何竟也学着说了一句："小蛮子。"

孩子们立即笑得东倒西歪。桑桑笑得屁股离开了凳子，凳子失去平衡，一头翘了起来，将坐在板凳那头的一个孩子掀倒在地上。那孩子跌了一脸的灰，心里想恼，但这时一直在擦黑板的蒋一轮转过身来："笑什么？安静！上课啦！"

Madam Qiu 2nd said, "I don't see him doing great in studies anyway. He might as well mess up in grade four."

Sang Qiao forced a smile and said, "Let me talk with teacher Jiang."

Xi Ma became Sang Sang's classmate.

When Xi Ma was presented to the class by Jiang Yilun, children all looked at him with curious and strange eyes. He was a little barbarian from a faraway place.

Xi Ma and Bald Crane shared a desk.

Xi Ma looked at Bald Crane's head and smiled, revealing his big front teeth.

Bald Crane said in a low voice, "Little barbarian!"

Xi Ma didn't understand him. He looked at him and around, as if asking, what the hell was the bald kid talking about?

The children all laughed.

Xi Ma didn't know what they were laughing about. But he felt he should just follow the others, so he laughed too.

Children laughed harder.

Bald Crane said again, "Little barbarian!"

Xi Ma still didn't know what he was talking about.

Children called in unison in a low voice, "Little barbarian!"

For whatever reason, Xi Ma copied them and said "Little barbarian" too.

Children laughed so hard that they could hardly keep their bodies straight. Sang Sang stood up; this caused the stool to lose its balance, making the kid sitting on the other end fall to the ground. The child had dust all over his face. He was irritated. Jiang Yilun, who had been wiping the blackboard, turned and said, "What's so funny? Be quiet. We are starting now!"

笑声这才渐渐平息下来。

课上了一阵，一直对细马的学习程度表示疑虑的蒋一轮打算再试一试细马，就让他站起来读课文。蒋一轮连说了三遍，这才使细马听明白老师是在让他念那篇课文。他吭哧了半天，把书捧起来，突然用很大的声音开始朗读。他的口音，与油麻地的口音实在相差太远了，油麻地的孩子们连一句都听不懂，只剩得一个叽里哇啦。

蒋一轮也几乎一句未能听懂。他试图想听懂，神情显得非常专注，但无济于事。听到后来，他先是觉得好笑，再接着就有点烦了。

细马直读得额上暴出青筋，脖子上的青筋更像吹足了气一样鼓了出来，满脸通红，并且一鼻头汗珠。

蒋一轮想摆手让他停下，可见他读得很卖力，又不忍让他停下。

孩子们就在下面笑，并且有人在不知什么意思的情况下，偶尔学着细马说一句，逗得大家大笑，转眼见到蒋一轮一脸不悦，才把笑声吞回肚里。

蒋一轮虽然听不懂，但蒋一轮能从细马的停顿、吭哧以及重复中听出，细马读这篇课文，是非常吃力的。

孩子们在下面不是偷偷地笑，就是交头接耳地说话，课堂里乱糟糟的。

蒋一轮终于摆了摆手，让细马停下，不要再读下去了。

细马从蒋一轮脸上明确地看到了失望。他不知想表达一个什么意思，反复地向蒋一轮重复着一句话。蒋一轮无法听

The classroom gradually calmed down.

After a few minutes, Jiang Yilun, who had been concerned with Xi Ma's level, intended to test him once again. He asked Xi Ma to stand up and read the textbook. Jiang Yilun had to give his order three times to get Xi Ma to understand what he was supposed to do. Xi Ma mumbled, held the textbook, and suddenly read it in a loud voice. His dialect was so different from that of Youmadi, that the children could hardly understand one single sentence.

Jiang Yilun didn't understand it either. He tried hard, looking very attentive, but to no avail. He felt funny and then got a bit fed up.

Xi Ma tried so hard that the veins on his forehead showed. The veins on his neck bulged like being blown full of air. His face was completely red and sweat hung on his nose.

Jiang Yilun wanted to wave to stop him. But he didn't do it, seeing how hard Xi Ma was trying.

The children all laughed. Occasionally someone mimicked a sentence of Xi Ma without knowing what it meant. All laughed. But when they saw the stern expression on Jiang Yilun's face, they stopped.

Although Jiang Yilun didn't understand Xi Ma, he could tell from Xi Ma's pauses, stammers and repetitions that it was extremely difficult for him.

Children either laughed secretly or chatted among themselves. The classroom was in disorder.

Finally Jiang Yilun waved to stop Xi Ma.

Xi Ma saw clearly the disappointment in Jiang Yilun's face. He said something to Jiang Yilun repeatedly, perhaps trying

懂，摇了一阵头，就用目光看孩子们，意思是：你们听懂了吗?下面的孩子全摇头。细马终于明白了:他被扔到了一个无法进行语言沟通的世界。他焦躁地看了看几十双茫然的眼睛，低下头去,感觉到了一个哑巴才有的那种压抑与孤单的心情。

蒋一轮摆了摆手，让细马坐了下去。

后来的时间里，细马就双目空空地看着黑板。

下了课，孩子们觉得自己憋了四十五分钟，终于有了说话的机会，不是大声地尖叫，就是互相用一种犹如一壶水烧沸了，壶盖儿噗噗噗地跳动的速度说话，整个校园，噪得听不清人语。

细马却独自一人靠在一棵梧桐树上,在无语的状态里想着江南的那个小镇、那个小学校、那些与他同操一种口音的孩子们。

下一节是算术课,细马又几乎一句未能听懂别人说的话。

第二天，细马一想到上课，心里就有点发憷，不想去上学了。但邱二爷不允许，他只好又不太情愿地来到学校。他越来越害怕讲话，一日一日地孤僻起来。过了七八天，他说什么也不肯去上学了。邱二爷想，耽误一两天，也没有什么，也就由他去了。但过了三四天，还不见他有上学的意思，就

to tell him something. Jiang Yilun didn't understand. He shook his head and looked at the children as if asking, did you understand? The children all shook their heads. Xi Ma finally realized that he had been thrown into a world where he couldn't communicate with others in his language. Anxiously, looked at dozens of empty eyes, he lowered his head, and felt the depression and isolation of the dumb.

Jiang Yilun waved to let Xi Ma sit down.

Xi Ma looked at the blackboard with empty eyes during the rest of the class.

Class was over. Children had been restrained for forty-five minutes, now they finally had an opportunity to talk. They either screamed or chatted with each other with tremendous speed -- it was as if water was boiling, and the cover of the kettle was shot up by the steam. The school was so abuzz that their words were unintelligible.

Xi Ma leaned on a Chinese parasol, alone. In his wordless world, he was thinking of the small town, the little school and the children speaking the same language, in the region south of the Yangtze River.

The next class was math. Xi Ma understood almost nothing.

The next day, Xi Ma was timid about going to school. He didn't want to go, but Old Qiu 2nd wouldn't agree, so Xi Ma reluctantly returned to school. He was afraid of speaking, and kept more and more to himself. Another seven or eight days passed, and then he wouldn't go to school no matter what. Old Qiu 2nd thought it was not important if he missed a couple of days' classes. So he let him stay home. But another three to four days passed, and Xi Ma still wouldn't go to school. Old

不答应了，将他拖到学校。当他被邱二爷硬推到教室门口，看到一屋子的孩子在一种出奇的寂静中看他时，他感到了一种更深刻的陌生，用双脚抵住门槛，赖着不肯进去，被邱二爷在后脑勺上猛击了一巴掌，加上蒋一轮伸过手去拉了他一下，他才坐回到秃鹤的身旁。

蒋一轮和其他所有老师，唯恐使细马感到难堪，就显得小心翼翼，不再在课堂上让细马站起来读书或发言。孩子们也不再笑他，只是在他不注意时悄悄地看着他，也不与他讲话。这样的局面，只是进一步强化了细马的孤单。

细马总是站在孩子群的外边，或是看着同学们做事，或是自己去另寻一件好玩的事情。

那天，桑桑回家对母亲说："细马总在田头上，与那群羊在一起玩。"

母亲就和桑桑一起来到院门口，朝田野上望去，只见细马坐在田埂上，那些羊正在他身边安闲地吃着草。那些羊仿佛已和细马很熟悉了，在他身边蹭来蹭去的，没有一只走远。

母亲说："和细马玩去吧。"

桑桑站着不动。因为，他和细马在一起时，总是觉得很生疏。无话可说，是件很难受的事情。不过，他还是朝细马走去了。

在一次小测验之后，细马又不来上学了。因为无法听懂老师的讲解，他的语文、算术成绩几乎就是零。那天，放了

Qiu 2nd dragged him to school. When Xi Ma was pushed to the door of the classroom, he saw everyone looking at him in extraordinary silence. He felt more profoundly that he was such a stranger. He pressed his legs against the threshold and just wouldn't go in. Old Qiu 2nd hit him on the back of his head abruptly, Jiang Yilun also stretched his hands out to pull him. Finally, Xi Ma sat down beside Bald Crane.

Jiang Yilun and all the other teachers worried that Xi Ma would feel embarrassed, so they became very careful to not ask him to stand up to recite, or to say anything. Children no longer laughed at him, just looked at him secretly when he wasn't taking any notice. They didn't speak to him. All these things aggregated Xi Ma's isolation.

Xi Ma always stood away from crowds of children, and just watched them doing things. He played on his own.

One day, Sang Sang went home and said to his mother, "Xi Ma is always in the field playing with the flock of sheep."

His mother came to the entrance of the courtyard with Sang Sang. She looked towards the field, and saw Xi Ma sitting on the low bank of the earth between fields, while sheep ate grass peacefully beside him. The sheep seemed to be quite comfortable with Xi Ma. They rubbed against him; none went away.

The mother said, "Go play with Xi Ma."

Sang Sang stood motionless. When he was with Xi Ma, he always felt distanced. It was painful, not having anything to say. But he still walked towards Xi Ma.

After a little quiz, Xi Ma once again refused to go to school. Because he didn't understand the lectures, he scored nearly zero in Chinese and math. After school, he didn't go home. He

学，他没有回家，直接去了田野上，走到羊群里。他坐下后，就再也没有动。

邱二爷喊他回去吃饭，他也不回。

邱二妈来到学校，问蒋一轮，细马在学校是犯错误了还是被人欺负了。蒋一轮就把小测验的结果告诉了她。邱二妈说："我看，这书念跟不念也差不多了。"

邱二爷也就没有再将细马拖回学校。他知道，细马原先在江南时就不是一个喜欢读书的孩子。他既然不肯读书，也就算了。

邱二妈对邱二爷说："你可得向他问清楚了，到底还读不读书，不要到以后说是我们不让他读书的。"

邱二爷走到田野上，来到细马身旁，问："你真的不想读书了？"

细马说："不想。"

"想好了？"

"想好了。"细马把一只羊搂住，也不看邱二爷一眼，回答说。

那天，邱二妈看到河边停了一条卖山羊的大船，就买下十只小山羊，对细马说："放羊去吧。"

2

每天早晨，当桑桑他们背着书包上学时，细马却赶着那十只山羊，到田野上牧羊去了。

went directly to the fields and walked among the sheep. He sat down and didn't move.

Old Qiu 2nd called him to have dinner. But he wouldn't move.

Madam Qiu 2nd came to school and asked Jiang Yilun whether Xi Ma had done anything wrong at school or had been bullied. Jiang Yilun told her the results of the quiz. She asked, "What's the point of his coming to school?"

Old Qiu 2nd didn't drag Xi Ma to school after that. He knew Xi Ma didn't like studying even when he was in his old home. If he didn't want to study, so be it.

Madam Qiu 2nd said to her husband, "You should have a word with Xi Ma; ask him whether he wants to study or not. I don't want him to say in the future that we didn't allow him to go to school."

Old Qiu 2nd walked to the fields and came to Xi Ma's side. He asked, "Do you really not want to go to school?"

Xi Ma said, "I don't want to go."

"Have you thought it through?"

"Yes." Xi Ma held a sheep. He didn't look at Old Qiu 2nd.

The other day, Madam Qiu 2nd saw a big ship selling goats docking at the riverside. She bought ten small goats and said to Xi Ma, "Go graze the goats!"

2

Every morning, when Sang Sang and others carried their bags to school, Xi Ma drove the ten goats to the fields to feed them.

细马好像还挺乐意。那十只小山羊，活蹦乱跳，一只只如同小精灵一般，一忽儿跑，一忽儿跳，一忽儿又互相打架，给细马带来了许多快乐。细马一面用一根树枝管着他们，一面不住地跟它们说话："走了，走了，我们吃草去了……多好的草呀，吃吧，吃吧，快点吃吧，再不吃，人家的羊就要来吃了……别再闹了，在草地上躺一会儿，晒晒太阳多好……你们再这样偷吃人家菜园里的草，被人家打了，我发誓，再也不管你们了……"细马觉得羊们是能听得懂他的话的，也只有羊能听得懂他的话。每逢想到这一点，细马就对油麻地小学的学生耿耿于怀：他们连我的话都听不懂；他们就不知道他们的话说得有多难听！他就在心中暗暗嘲笑他们读课文时那种腔调：说的什么话呀，一个个都是大舌头，一个个好像都堵了一鼻孔鼻涕！

细马似乎很喜欢这儿的天地。那么大，那么宽广的大平原。到处是庄稼和草木，到处是飞鸟与野兔什么的。有那么多条大大小小的河，有那么多条大大小小的船。他喜欢看鱼鹰捕鱼，喜欢听远处的牛哞哞长叫，喜欢看几个猎人带了几只长腿细身的猎狗在麦地或棉花地里追捕兔子，喜欢听芦苇丛里一种水鸟有一声无一声地很哀怨地鸣叫，喜欢看风车在野风里发狂似的旋转……他就在这片田野上，带着他的羊，或干脆将它们暂时先放下不管，到处走。一切都是有趣的。他乐意去做许多事情：追逐一条狗，在小水塘里捉几条鱼，发现了一个黄鼠狼的洞，就用竹片往洞的深处挖……

He seemed to be pleased. Then ten little goats were very active. Like little spirits, they ran and jumped, fought each other, giving Xi Ma a lot of pleasure. Xi Ma disciplined them with a branch, while talking with them all the time, "Go, go, let's get some grass... Such great grass. Eat, eat, hurry up. If you don't hurry up, other sheep and goats will come... Don't be naughty. Lie on the grass for a while. Isn't it great to bathe in the sun... Don't eat the grass in others' gardens. If you do this and get beaten, I swear I won't care..." Xi Ma felt the goats understood what he said. Only the goats understood his words. Whenever he thought of it, Xi Ma bore a grudge against Youmadi pupils. They didn't even understand my words. They didn't know how unpleasant their dialect sounded! Xi Ma laughed secretly at the tone of pupils reading textbooks. What they were talking about? They all had big tongues, and they spoke as if their noses were blocked by mucus.

But Xi Ma liked his surroundings. It was such a big and wide plain. There were crops, grass and trees everywhere, and birds and hares. There were so many rivers big and small, boats big and small. He liked to watch fish hawks catching fish, to listen to the lowing of cattle in the distance, to watch hunters with long-legged slim-bodied hounds chasing hares in the wheat and cotton fields, to listen to the on and off miserable cries of water birds in the reed bushes, to see the crazy rotating of the windmill...He spent his time in the fields with his goats. Sometimes, he wandered around, leaving the goats alone for a while. Everything was interesting to him. He loved to do things -- chase a dog, catch fish in the small pond, find the yellow weasel's hole and dig into it with a piece of bamboo ...

这样过了一些日子，细马忽然觉得这一切又不再有什么趣味了。当他听到从油麻地小学传来的读书声、吵闹声时，他就会站在田野上，向油麻地小学长久地张望。然而，他又不愿意再回到学校读书。

冬天到了，因为平原没有什么遮拦，北风总是长驱直入，在原野上肆无忌惮地乱扑乱卷。细马虽然不必天天将羊们赶到田野上，但他得常常拿一把小镰刀去河坡、田埂上割那些已经枯萎了的草或漏割的豆秸，然后背回来喂羊。北风像冰碴儿一般锐利地划着他的手、他的脸。没有几天，他的手就裂口了，露出红艳艳的肉来。晚上，邱二妈烧一盆热水，邱二爷就把细马拉过来，让他将双手放在热水里长时间地浸泡，然后擦干，再让他涂上蛤蜊油。但即使这样，细马的手仍在北风中不时地产生出一种切割样的疼痛。每逢此时，他就对那些坐在门上挂了厚厚草帘的教室中读书的孩子们产生出一种嫉妒，一种敌意。

冬天过去，细马已基本上能听得懂油麻地人“难听的”话了。但，细马依然没有去学校上学。一是因为邱二妈并未提出让他再去读书，二是细马觉得，自己落了一个学期的课，跟是不可能再跟上了，除非留级，而细马不愿意这样丢人。细马还是放他的羊，虽然细马心里并不喜欢放羊。

细马越来越喜欢将羊群赶到离油麻地小学比较近的地方来放。现在，他不在乎油麻地小学的孩子们用异样的目光来

After living like this for some time, Xi Ma suddenly felt it was no longer interesting. When he heard reading and other sounds from Youmadi school, he stood in the fields and looked for a long time at the school. But he didn't want to go back.

Winter came. The north wind drove straight in -- there was nothing on the plain to deter it. The wind attacked the plain and swept things rampantly and relentlessly. Xi Ma didn't have to graze the goats everyday in the fields. But he still had to take his sickle to the slope near the river and low banks of earth between fields, to cut withered grass or beanstalks left there uncut, and carry them home to feed the goats. The north wind beat his hands and face sharply like ice. In only a few days, Xi Ma's hands cracked and the flesh beneath his the skin was exposed. In the evening, Madam Qiu 2nd heated a pot of water. Old Qiu 2nd pulled Xi Ma over and put his hands in the hot water for a long time. He then dried Xi Ma's hands and applied clam oil to them. Even so, in the north wind, Xi Ma's hands still gave him constant, piercing pain. At times like that, Xi Ma became hostile, and envious of the kids studying in classrooms protected by a thick straw curtain.

After winter, Xi Ma could almost understand the "unpleasant" Youmadi dialect. But he still didn't go to school. Madam Qiu 2nd didn't mention it. And Xi Ma felt it was impossible for him to catch up since he had missed one term's classes, unless he studied with a lower grade. But Xi Ma didn't want to lose face. He still grazed his goats, although he didn't enjoy it any more.

Xi Ma liked more and more to drive the goats near to Youmadi school to feed them. He didn't care about those strange

看他。他甚至喜欢挑战性地用自己那双眍眼去与那些目光对视，直至那些目光忽然觉得有点发虚而不再去看他。他在油麻地首先学会的是骂人的话，并且是一些不堪入耳的骂人的话。他知道，这些骂人的话，最能侮辱对方，也最能伤害和刺激对方。当一个孩子向他的羊群投掷泥块，或走过来逗弄他的羊，他就会去骂他们。他之所以骂他们，一是表明他讨厌他们，二是表明他现在也能讲油麻地的话了。油麻地的孩子们都已感觉到，这个江南小蛮子是一个很野蛮的孩子。知道了这一点，也就没有太多的孩子去招惹他。这使细马很失望。他希望有人来招惹他，然后他好去骂他们。他甚至在内心渴望着跟油麻地小学的某一个孩子狠狠地打一架。

孩子们看出了这一点，就更加小心地躲避着他。

细马就把羊群赶到油麻地小学的孩子们上学必须经过的路口。他让他的羊在路上拉屎撒尿。女孩子们既怕羊，又怕他，就只好从田里走。男孩子们不怕，硬是要走过来。这时若惊动了他的羊，他就要骂人。如果那个挨骂的男孩不答应他的无理，要上来与他打架，他就会感到十分兴奋，立即迎上去，把身体斜侧给对方，昂着头说："想打架吗？"那个男孩就有可能被他这股挑衅的气势吓住，就会显得有点畏缩。他就会对那个男孩说："有种的就打我一拳！"有几个男孩动手了，但都发现细马是一个非常有力气的孩子，加上他在打架时所表现出的凶样，纠缠了一阵，见着机会，就赶紧摆脱了他，逃掉了事。六年级有一个男孩仗着自己身高力大，不怕他的凶样，故意过来踢了一只羊的屁股。细马骂了一句，就

eyes looking at him anymore. He even stared back with a challenge in his sunken eyes, until people avoided his gaze. The first words of the local dialect he learned were cursing ones, and dirty words at that. He knew the words that could best insult others, hurt or provoke them. If someone threw mud at his flock, or came over to play with his goats, he would curse the guy. He wanted to show that he disliked people, and now he could speak the local dialect. Youmadi children all felt that this little southern brat was a very barbaric child; very few kids bothered him. Xi Ma was disappointed. He wanted people to bother him, so that he could curse back. He even desired to have a serious fight with one of the Youmadi children.

Youmadi children understood this, so carefully avoided him.

Xi Ma drove his flock to the junction where Youmadi children had to pass to go to school. He let his goats relieve themselves on the road. Girls were afraid of the goats and Xi Ma, and they had to walk around, in the fields. Boys were not in awe of him, and they just walked on the road. If someone startled his goats, Xi Ma would curse. If the subject of his cursing felt indignant and came to pick a fight with him, Xi Ma would get aroused. He would come up immediately, tilt his body towards his opponent, raise his head and say, "Do you want to fight?" The boy would be frightened by his challenge and look a bit diminished. Xi Ma would then say to him, "If you have the guts, hit me! " A few boys did hit him, but they found Xi Ma very strong, and he looked really fierce. After a few scuffles, boys found an opportunity to get rid of Xi Ma. There was a boy from grade six who was tall and strong. He was not afraid of Xi Ma and one day deliberately kicked the bottom of a goat. Xi Ma

冲了过去。那个男孩揪住他的衣服，用力甩了他两个圆圈，然后双手一松，细马就往后倒去，最后跌坐在地上。细马顺手操起两块砖头。

两个小孩打架打急了眼，从地上抓砖头要砸人的有的是，但十有八九是拿着砖头吓唬人。砖头倒是抓得很紧，但并不敢砸出去。胆大的知道对方不敢砸，就在那里等他过来。这一方就抓着砖头奔过来了，把砖头扬起来。胆大的也有点害怕，但还是大声地说："你敢砸我！你敢砸我！"抓砖头的这一个就说："我就敢砸你！"嘴硬，但末了也不敢砸。胆大的也有点发虚，怕万一真的砸出来，就走开了。

但细马却是来真的。他对准那个高个子男孩，就扔出去一块砖头。那高个儿男孩一躲闪，就听见砖头刷的从他的耳边飞了过去。眼见着细马拿了砖头冲过来，一副绝对真干的样子，男孩吓得掉头直往校园里跑。细马又从地上捡了一块砖，一手提一块，并不猛追，咬着牙走进了校园。吓得高个男孩到处乱窜，最后竟然藏到女生厕所里，把前来上厕所的几个女孩子吓得哇哇乱叫。细马没有找到那个高个男孩，就提着砖头走到校园外面，坐在路上，一直守到放学。高个男孩回不去家，只好跑到小河边上，让一个放鸭子的老头用船把他送过河去。

油麻地小学的老师就交待各班同学：不要去惹细马。

cursed him and charged over. The boy grabbed Xi Ma by his clothes, spun him around twice, then dropped him. Xi Ma fell backward to the ground. He picked up two rocks.

When two kids were in the heat of a fight, one often picked up rocks or bricks and threatened to hit the other, but mostly this was just for show, to frighten the other. He would grab the bricks solidly, but wouldn't throw them. If the other party had courage, and knew his opponent wouldn't really throw the bricks, he would stand there waiting. The boy with the bricks would pretend to attack, holding his weapons high. The other would be a bit afraid, but would scream,"I dare you to hit me! I dare you!" The one with the bricks would say, "Just wait to see me hit you!" But he was just pretending and wouldn't hit. The other would become intimidated, worrying that he would indeed be hit, so he would just walk away.

But now Xi Ma meant it. He threw one brick at the tall boy; he boy dodged it, and heard the brick fly past his ear. He saw Xi Ma charging over with another brick and looking serious. Frightened, the tall boy turned and ran to the school ground. Xi Ma picked up another brick from the ground, now one brick in each hand. He didn't chase him, but just walked in the schoolyard with clenched teeth. The tall boy was so frightened he ran all over the school to escape. Finally he hid himself in the girls' toilet. The few girls in the toilet screamed. Xi Ma couldn't find the tall boy. He took his bricks and walked outside the school grounds, waiting for the tall boy until school was over. The boy couldn't go home. He had to run to the riverside and ask the old man feeding the ducks to row him across the river.

Teachers told pupils not to bother Xi Ma.

但秃鹤还是去惹了细马。结果，两人就在路上打起来了。秃鹤打不过细马，被细马骑在身上足有一个小时。细马就是不肯放开他。有人去喊蒋一轮。蒋一轮过来，连说带拉，才把细马弄开。秃鹤鼻子里流着血，哭丧着脸跑了。

傍晚，桑乔找了邱二爷与邱二妈，说了细马的事。

晚上，邱二妈就将细马骂了一顿。细马在挨骂时，就用割草的镰刀，一下子一下子往乌桕树上砍，将乌桕树砍了许多眼。邱二妈过来，将镰刀夺下，扔进了菜园，就对邱二爷嚷嚷："谁让你将他带回来的!"

邱二爷过来，打了一下细马的后脑勺："吃饭去!"

细马不吃饭，鞋都不脱，上了自己的床，把被子蒙在头上哭。哭着哭着，就睡着了。

邱二妈从一开始就觉得，细马不是一个一般的孩子。她从他的眍眼里看出，这已是一个有了心机的孩子。当她这样认为时，细马在她眼里就不再是一个孩子，而是一个大人了。现在这个大人冲着他们的一笔家产突然地来了。邱二妈从一开始，就对细马是排斥的。

五月的一天，邱二妈终于对细马叫了起来："你回去吧，你明天就回你家去!"

事情的发生与桑桑有关。

这是一个星期天，细马正在放羊，桑桑过来了。现在，

But Bald Crane still tormented him. The two fought on the road. Bald Crane wasn't up to Xi Ma, and he was sat on by Xi Ma for an entire hour. Xi Ma would not let him go. Someone called Jiang Yilun over, who talked and pulled and finally got Xi Ma off. Bald Crane's nose bled, and he ran away, looking very distressed.

At dusk, Sang Qiao found Old Qiu 2nd and Madam Qiu 2nd and told them what had happened.

In the evening, Madam Qiu 2nd scolded Xi Ma hard. Xi Ma chopped the tallow tree with his sickle while being scolded by Madam Qiu 2nd. He chopped and there left many wounds on the tree. Madam Qiu 2nd took the sickle from him and threw it to the vegetable garden. She shouted at her husband, "Why the hell did you bring him here?"

Old Qiu 2nd came over and struck Xi Ma on the back of his head. He said, "Go have supper!"

Xi Ma didn't eat. He went to bed without taking off his shoes. He covered his head with a quilt and cried, and finally went to sleep.

From the beginning, Madam Qiu 2nd thought Xi Ma was no ordinary child. She saw in his sunken eyes that the child had his own ideas. He was no longer a child in her eyes, but a grown-up, who suddenly descended upon them, looking for their fortune. Madam Qiu 2nd had rejected Xi Ma from the beginning.

One day in May, Madam Qiu 2nd finally shouted to Xi Ma, "Go home. Go back to your home tomorrow."

It had something to do with Sang Sang.

One Sunday, Xi Ma was grazing his goats and Sang Sang came over. Sang Sang was the closest thing to a friend that Xi

桑桑几乎是细马唯一的朋友。桑桑和细马在田野上玩耍时，桑桑说："我们去镇上玩吧。"

细马说："去。"

桑桑和细马丢下那群羊，就去镇上了。两人在镇上一人买了一块烧饼，一边吃，一边逛，到吃午饭的时间了，还没有想起来回家。又逛了一阵，正想回家，桑桑看到天上有群鸽子落在一个人家的房顶上。桑桑见了鸽子，就迈不开腿，拉了细马，就去那个人家看鸽子。也就是看鸽子。但桑桑光看，就能看得忘了自己。细马对谁都凶，可就是很顺从桑桑。他就蹲在墙根下，陪着桑桑。主人见两个孩子看他们家的鸽子，一看就是一两个小时，心里就生了疑，过来打量他俩。细马碰了碰桑桑的胳膊。桑桑看到了一对多疑的目光，这才和细马匆匆走出镇子往家走。

在细马离开羊群的这段时间里，羊吃了人家半条田埂的豆苗。

邱二妈向人家赔了礼，将羊赶回羊圈里。

细马回来了。他很饿，就直奔厨房，揭了锅盖，盛了满满一大碗饭，正准备坐在门槛上扒饭，邱二妈来了："你还好意思吃饭？"

细马端着碗，不知是吃好还是不吃好。

Ma had. They played in the fields and then Sang Sang said, "Let's go to the town."

Xi Ma said, "OK."

They left the goats and went to town. They each bought a sesame seed cake, eating it while looking around. It was time for lunch, but they didn't think of going home. They strolled in the town for another while and meant to go home. But then Sang Sang saw a flock of pigeons falling on the rooftop of a household. Whenever Sang Sang saw pigeons, he wouldn't leave. He pulled Xi Ma and went to look at the pigeons. Sang Sang forgot himself looking at the pigeons. Xi Ma was fierce to everyone else, but he was tame with Sang Sang. He squatted at the corner of the wall, keeping Sang Sang company. The owner saw two kids looking at his pigeons, and when they had been there for a couple of hours, he got suspicious and came to see what they were up to. Xi Ma touched Sang Sang's arm. Sang Sang saw the pair of suspicious eyes and hastened back home with Xi Ma.

During the time Xi Ma left the goats alone, they ate someone's other's bean seedlings, planted on a low bank of earth between fields.

Madam Qiu 2nd apologized and drove the flock back to the pen.

Xi Ma came home. He was hungry so he ran to the kitchen directly. He opened the cover of the pan and filled his bowl high with rice. He was about to sit on the threshold to have his rice when Madam Qiu 2nd came. She said, "Aren't you ashamed, eating?"

Xi Ma held the bowl, wasn't sure whether he should eat or not.

“你吃饭倒是挺能吃的，才多大一个人，一顿能扒尖尖两碗饭！可让你干点活，就难了！你放羊放到哪儿去了？我告诉你，我们养不起你！”邱二妈说完，去桑桑家了。

细马端着碗，眼泪就流了下来，泪珠啪嗒啪嗒地掉在饭碗里。他突然转过身，把饭碗搁到了灶台上，走出了厨房，来到屋后。

屋后是邱二爷家的自留地。一地的麦子刚刚割完，一捆捆麦子，都还搁在地里，未扛回院子里。

细马下地，扛了一捆麦子，就往院子里走。他扛了一捆又一捆，一刻也不停歇。

当时是下午四点，阳光还在强烈地照射着平原。细马汗淋淋地背着麦捆，脸被晒得通红。几道粗粗的汗痕，挂在脸上。他脱掉了褂子，露出光脊梁。太阳的照晒，麦芒的刺戳，加上汗水的腌泡，使他觉得浑身刺挠，十分难受，但细马一直背着麦捆，一声不吭。

桑桑的母亲见到了，就过来说：“细马，别背了。”

细马没有回答，继续背下去。

桑桑的母亲就过来拉细马，细马却挣脱了。她望着细马的背影说：“你这孩子，也真犟！”

邱二妈走过来说：“师娘，你别管他，由他去。”

桑桑来了。母亲给了他一巴掌：“就怪你。”

"You do eat a lot! You are still a child but you have two bowls of rice at each meal. But what about your work? Where have you been? I tell you, we cannot feed you!" Madam Qiu 2nd finished and went to Sang Sang's.

Xi Ma held the bowl and tears dripped into it. He turned abruptly and put the bowl on the top of stove. He walked out of the kitchen and went to the back room.

At the Qiu family's plot, wheat had just been cut and bundles of wheat were left on the ground. They had yet to be carried back to the courtyard.

Xi Ma picked up a bundle of wheat and walked to the courtyard. He carried bundle after bundle, without taking a moment's rest.

It was four o'clock in the afternoon. The sun shone relentlessly on the plain. Xi Ma carried bundles of wheat and was sweating all over; his face was red. A few lines of thick sweat hung on his face. He took off his shirt, exposing his bare back. The sun shone on him, the wheat awn pricked him, and the sweat soaked him; all these made him itch all over. He was extremely uncomfortable, but he just went on carrying wheat bundles, without a word.

Sang Sang's mother saw him and came over. "Xi Ma, leave it."

Xi Ma didn't answer. He just went on.

Sang Sang's mother came to pull from his task, but he got rid of her. She looked at the back of Xi Ma and said, "What a child, so stubborn!"

Madam Qiu 2nd came over and said, "Madam Sang, don't you mind him, just let him alone."

Sang Sang came over. His mother struck him and said, "It's all your fault."

桑桑也下地了，他要帮细马，也扛起麦捆来。

桑桑的母亲回家忙了一阵子事,出来看到细马还在背麦捆，就又过来叫细马：“好细马，听我话，别背了。”

桑桑也过来：“细马，别背了。”

细马抹了一把汗，摇了摇头。

桑桑的母亲就一把拉住他。桑桑也过来帮母亲推他。细马就拼命挣扎，要往地里去，眼睛里流出一两行泪水，喉咙里呜咽着。三个人就在地头纠缠着。

邱二妈叫着：“你回去吧，你明天就回你家去!”

桑桑的母亲就回过头来：“二妈，你也别生气，就别说什么了。”

这时，邱二爷从外面回来了，听桑桑的母亲说了一些情况，说：“还不听师娘劝!”

细马却仍然挣扎着，企图挣出桑桑和他母亲的手。

这时走来了桑乔。他没有动手：“你们把他放了。细马，我说话有用吗?”

被桑桑和他母亲松开了的细马，站在那儿，不住地用手背擦眼泪。

桑乔这才过来拉住细马的手：“来，先到我家去，我们谈谈。”

邱二爷说：“听桑校长的话，跟桑校长走。”

细马就被桑乔拉走了。

Sang Sang went to the plot too, to help Xi Ma carry the wheat bundles.

Sang Sang's mother went home and got busy. When she came back, she saw Xi Ma still carrying wheat bundles. She called him, "Good old Xi Ma, listen to me. Give it up."

Sang Sang came over too, "Xi Ma, that's enough."

Xi Ma wiped his sweat and shook his head.

Sang Sang's mother grabbed him. Sang Sang helped her push Xi Ma too. Xi Ma struggled hard to go to back to the plot, tears dripping down his face. He sobbed. The three tangled at the edge of the plot.

Madam Qiu 2nd shouted, "Go home, you go back to your home tomorrow!"

Sang Sang's mother turned, "Madam Qiu 2nd, don't be angry with him. Don't say anything."

Old Qiu 2nd came back home. He heard what had happed from Sang Sang's mother and asked, "Why didn't you listen to Madam Sang?"

Xi Ma still struggled to get free from of Sang Sang and his mother.

Sang Qiao came. He didn't raise his hands. He just said, "Let go of Xi Ma. Xi Ma, would you listen to me?"

Sang Sang and his mother let go of Xi Ma, who stood there and constantly wiped tears with the back of his hands.

Sang Qiao came to grab Xi Ma's hand, "Come to my home. Let's talk."

Old Qiu 2nd said, "Listen to principal Sang, go with principal Sang."

Sang Qiao pulled him away.

这里，邱二妈哭了起来："师娘，我命苦哇……"

桑桑的母亲就劝她回去，别站在地头。

邱二妈倚在地头的一棵树上，哭着说着："他才这么大一点的人，我就一句说不得了。等他长大了，我们还能指望得上他吗？"

桑桑的母亲劝了邱二妈半天，才把她劝回家。

当天晚上，细马就住在桑桑家。

3

细马确实是一个很有主意的男孩。他已暗暗准备离开油麻地，回他的江南老家。他去办户口的地方，想先把自己的户口迁出来。但人家笑话他："一个小屁孩子，也来迁户口。"根本不理他。他就在那里软磨硬抗。管户口的人见他不走，便说："我要去找你家的大人。"他怕邱二爷知道他的计划，这才赶紧走掉。他也曾打算不管他的户口了，就这么走了再说，但无奈自己又没有路费。现在，他已开始积攒路费。他把在放羊时捉的鱼或摸的螺蛳卖得的钱，把邱二爷给他买糖块的钱，全都悄悄地藏在床下的一只小瓦罐里。

当然，细马在暗暗进行这一计划时，也是时常犹豫的。因为，他已越来越感到邱二爷是喜欢他的，并且越来越喜欢。

Madam Qiu 2nd cried, "Madam Sang, I'm so frustrated..."

Sang Sang's mother persuaded her to go back from the edge of the plot.

Madam Qiu 2nd leaned on a tree and cried, "He is just a child. But he gets mad with just a few words of mine. When he grows up, can we really rely on him?"

Sang Sang's mother reasoned with Madam Qiu 2nd for a long time before taking her home.

Xi Ma stayed with the Sang's in the evening.

3

Xi Ma was indeed a boy of ideas. He had secretly begun to prepare for his departure from Youmadi, to go back to his hometown. He went to the registration office and wanted to take out his papers. But people there laughed at him, "You are still a kid, how can you transfer your registration?" They ignored him. He wouldn't leave, and the people were annoyed. One said, "I'm going to look for your parents." Xi Ma worried that Old Qiu 2nd would find out what he was up too, so he left the registration office in a hurry. He thought he could forget about his registration papers and just leave. But he didn't have any money to pay for the journey. So he began to save money. While grazing his goats, he caught fish and snails and sold them. He also saved the money Old Qui 2nd gave him for candies. He hid all the money in a small pottery tank under the bed.

Of course, Xi Ma had hesitations too, as he secretly proceeded with his plan. He felt more and more that Old Qiu

他不会游泳，而这里到处是河。邱二爷怕他万一掉进河里——这种机会对于生活在这里的人来说，也实在太多了——就教他学游泳。邱二爷站在水中，先是双手托着他的肚皮，让他在水中扑腾，然后，仅用一只手托住他的下巴，引他往前慢慢地游动。一连几天，邱二爷就这么耐心地教他。邱二爷是好脾气。细马终于可以脱开邱二爷的手，向前游动了，虽然还很笨拙，还很吃力，仅仅能游出去丈把远。那天，邱二爷在河边坐着，看着他游，后来想起一件什么事来，让细马不要游远了，就暂时回去了。细马突然起了要跟邱二爷淘气一下的心思，看着邱二爷的背影，悄悄躲到了水边的芦苇丛里。邱二爷惦记着水中的细马，很快返回，见水面上没有细马，一惊："细马!细马……"见无人答应，眼前只是一片寂静的水面，邱二爷又大喊了一声"细马"，就纵身跳进水中。他发了疯地在水中乱抓乱摸。在水底下实在憋不住了，才冒出水面："细马!细马……"他慌乱地叫着，声音带着哭腔。细马钻出芦苇丛，朝又一次从水底冒出来的邱二爷露出了大门牙，笑着。邱二爷浑身颤抖不已。他过来，揪住细马的耳朵，将他揪到了岸上，然后操起一根棍子，砸着细马的屁股。这是细马来到油麻地以后，邱二爷第一次揍他——第一次揍就

2nd liked him. Xi Ma didn't know how to swim. There were rivers everywhere here. Old Qiu 2nd was afraid that Xi Ma might fall in the river -- it was a big possibility for people living there. So Old Qiu 2nd taught Xi Ma to swim. He stood in the water, supported Xi Ma's belly with his hands, and let Xi Ma kick in the water. Then Old Qiu 2nd held Xi Ma's chin with one hand, and led him slowly forward. For days in a row, Old Qiu 2nd patiently coached Xi Ma. He was really good-tempered. Finally Xi Ma could let go of Old Qiu 2nd's hand and swim alone, although he was still awkward and struggling, and he could only swim for a few zhangs. One day, Old Qiu 2nd sat on the riverside and watched Xi Ma swimming. He thought of something and asked Xi Ma not to swim too far away, and he went home for a while. Xi Ma suddenly wanted to be naughty. He saw the back of Old Qiu 2nd and hid in the reed bushes near the bank. Old Qiu 2nd worried about Xi Ma and came back quickly. He didn't see Xi Ma and panicked. He shouted, "Xi Ma! Xi Ma..." there was no answer. There only a stretch of quiet water surface. Old Qiu 2nd shouted "Xi Ma!" again and jumped in the water. He grabbed and probed in the river crazily. He dove and didn't come up until he couldn't hold his breath anymore. He shouted "Xi Ma! Xi Ma..." anxiously and shakily. Then Xi Ma came out from the reed bushes and grinned with his big front teeth at Old Qiu 2nd, who then came out of the water. Old Qiu 2nd was shaking. He came out, grabbed Xi Ma by his ears and pulled him to the embankment. He grabbed a stick to thrash Xi Ma on his buttocks. This was the first time Old Qiu 2nd had beat him since he had come to Youmadi, and he beat Xi Ma really hard.

揍得这么狠。细马哭了起来，邱二爷这才松手。细马看到邱二爷好像也哭了。这天深夜，细马觉得有人来到了他的床边。他半睁开眼睛，看到邱二爷端着一盏小油灯，正低头查看着他被棍子砸过的屁股。邱二爷走了。他看着昏暗的灯光映照下的邱二爷的背影消失在门口，然后闭上双眼。不一会儿，就有泪珠从眼缝里挤了出来。

细马想起，邱二爷去江南向他的父亲提出想要一个孩子，而他的父亲决定让邱二爷将他带走时，邱二爷并没有嫌他太小，而是欢喜地将一只粗糙的大手放在他的脑袋上，仿佛他此次来，要的就是他。而当他听父亲说要将他送给二叔时，他也没有觉得什么，仿佛这是一件早商量好了的事情。他在那只大手下站着，直觉得那只大手是温暖的……

细马甚至也不在心里恨邱二妈。除了与他隔膜和冷淡，邱二妈实际上对任何人都显得十分温和、和善。谁家缺米了，她会说："到我家先量几升米吃吧。"若是一个已经借过米但还未还的，不好意思来，她就会量个三升五升的米，主动送上人家的门："到收了稻子再还吧。"桑桑的母亲要纳一家人的鞋底，邱二妈就会对桑桑的母亲说："让我帮你纳两双。"她纳的鞋底，针线又密又紧，鞋底板得像块铁，十分结实。桑桑脚上穿的鞋，鞋底差不多都是邱二妈纳的。

但细马还是计划着走。

Xi Ma cried and Old Qiu 2nd stopped. Xi Ma saw Old Qui 2nd crying too. Late in the night, Xi Ma felt someone coming to his bed. He half-opened his eyes and saw Old Qiu 2nd holding a small oil lamp and checking carefully his buttocks which he had struck earlier. Xi Ma saw the back of Old Qiu 2nd in the dim light disappearing at the door, and closed his eyes. After a while, he started crying.

Xi Ma remembered when Old Qiu 2nd had come to his home and asked his father for a child, and his father had given him away . Old Qui 2nd didn't care that Xi Ma was too young. He put a big coarse hand on Xi Ma's head affectionately, it was as if he had meant to take Xi Ma. When Xi Ma heard from his father that he was to be given away to his second uncle, he didn't feel anything special, as if it were a thing decided long ago. He had stood under Old Qiu 2nd's big hand and felt it was really warm...

Xi Ma didn't even hate Madam Qiu 2nd in his heart. Apart from her distance and cold to him, she was in fact quite gentle and kind to all people. If someone ran out of rice, she would say, "Come to my home to get a few shengs." If the person had borrowed rice from the Qius and had not returned it, he would be too ashamed to come. Madam Qiu 2nd would measure three to five shengs of rice and deliver the rice herself to his door. She would say, "You can return it to us after the harvest." Sang Sang's mother had to stitch soles for the whole family, and Madam Qiu 2nd would say, "Let me stitch a couple for you." The soles she made had very dense and tight stitches, as solid as iron. All the shoes Sang Sang wore had soles stitched by her.

But Xi Ma still planned to go.

夏天过去之后，细马与邱二妈又发生了一次激烈的冲突。邱二妈向邱二爷大哭："你必须马上将他送走！"

邱二爷是老实人。邱二爷与邱二妈成家之后，一般都听邱二妈的。他们家，是邱二妈作主，邱二爷只是随声附和而已。他想想细马在油麻地生活得也不快活，也不想再为难细马了，就对细马说："你要回去，就回去吧。"他去把细马的户口迁了出来。

这以后的好几天，邱二妈总不说话。因为，当她终于知道，细马真的马上要离去时，她心中又有另一番说不清楚的感觉了。她甚至觉得，她原来并不是多么地不喜欢细马。她在给细马收拾东西时，收拾着收拾着，就会突然停住，然后很茫然地望着那些东西。

说好了这一天送细马走的。但就在要送他走的头两天，天气忽然大变。一天一夜的狂风暴雨，立即给平原蒙上了涝灾的阴影。原以为隔一两天，天会好起来，但后来竟然一连七八天都雨水不绝。或倾盆大雨，或滴滴答答地下个不止，七八天里，太阳没有出来过一分钟。河水一天一天地在涨高，现在已经漫上岸来。稻田已被淹没，到处白茫茫。地势高一些的稻田，只能看见少许稻叶在水面上无奈地摇曳。

道路都没有了。细马暂时走不了。细马似乎也不急着走了。望着止不住的雨水，他并无焦急的样子。

桑桑这几天，总和细马在一起。他们好像很喜欢这样的天气。他们各人拿了一根木棍，在水中试探着被水淹掉了的

After summer, Xi Ma had another heated conflict with Madam Qiu 2nd, who cried at her husband, "You have to send him away immediately!"

Old Qiu 2nd was a simple man. Since getting married, he had always listened to his wife. She decided everything in the household, and Old Qiu 2nd just echoed her. He thought Xi Ma wasn't happy in Youmadi, and he didn't want to make things difficult for him. So he told Xi Ma, "If you want to go back, go." He took out his registration paper.

In the following days, Madam Qiu 2nd didn't speak. When she finally realized that Xi Ma was to go, she had a feeling of confusion. She even felt it was not entirely true that she didn't like Xi Ma. As she packed for him, she would suddenly stop and look at his things in a loss.

The day to send Xi Ma away was fixed. But two days before that day, the weather suddenly changed. A violent storm lasted for a day and a night, threatening to flood the plain. People thought it would get better after a couple of days, but the rain didn't stop for seven or eight days. It was either pouring or an incessant drizzle. The sun didn't come out for a single minute. The river rose day after day and began to overfill. The rice fields were flooded. There was an expanse of water everywhere. For those rice fields on higher ground, only a few rice stalks were seen swaying hopelessly on the water surface.

The roads were gone. Xi Ma couldn't go anywhere. He didn't seem to be eager. Seeing the non-stop, he wasn't impatient to go.

Sang Sang was always with Xi Ma those days. They seemed to like this kind of weather. They each held a wooden stick and explored the flooded road. They walked ahead step by

路，一步一步地往前走，觉得非常有趣。两人一不小心，就会走到路外边，滑到比路基低得多的缺口或池塘里，弄得一身湿淋淋的。细马回到家，邱二妈就赶紧让他换上干衣。细马换了干衣，禁不住外头桑桑的召唤，又拿了木棍试探着，走出门去。这时，邱二妈就在家点起火，将细马刚换下的衣服晾在铁丝上，慢慢烘烤着。这时，邱二妈就在心里想：马上，细马又要湿淋淋地回来了。

雨根本没有停息的意思。天空低垂，仿佛最后一颗太阳已经永远地飘逝，从此，天地间将陷入绵延无穷的黑暗。雨大时，仿佛天河漏底，厚厚实实的雨幕，遮挡住了一切：树木、村庄……就只剩下了这厚不见底的雨幕。若是风起，这雨飘飘洒洒，犹如巨瀑。空气一天一天紧张起来。到处在筑坝、围堤。坝中又有坝，堤中又有堤，好像在准备随时往后撤退。桑桑和细马撑着小船，去看过一次大坝。他们看见至少有二十只从上面派来的抽水机船，正把水管子搁在大坝上，往外抽水。那一排水管，好似一门一门大炮，加上机器的一片轰鸣和水声，倒让桑桑和细马激动了半天。随时会听到报警的锣声。人们听到锣声，就说："不知哪儿又决口了。"

油麻地小学自然属于这地方的重点保护单位，早已将它连同一片住户围在了坝里。这坝外面还有更大范围的坝。

step and felt it interesting. Whenever they were a bit careless, they would reach the edge of the road, and fall into a crack or a pond much lower than the roadbed, getting completely soaked. When Xi Ma got home, Madam Qiu 2nd would hurry to let him change and put on dry clothes. Xi Ma put on dry clothes, but Sang Sang was calling him from outside. Xi Ma couldn't resist and took his wooden stick, tested the water and walked out again. Madam Qiu 2nd set up a fire at home, put the wet clothes on wires to dry them slowly. But she knew he would come back completely wet again.

The rain was not going to stop. The sky was low, as if the last sun had gone forever, and it would be eternal darkness. When the rain was heavy, it was as if the river in the heavens had a leaking bed. The thick and solid rain curtain covered everything -- trees, villages... There was only the thick, bottomless rain curtain. When the wind blew, the rain floated like a gigantic waterfall. The atmosphere got tenser day after day. People were building dams and embankments everywhere. There were dams on dams, and embankments on embankments, as if people were prepared to retreat anytime. Sang Sang and Xi Ma punted a boat to see the big dam one day. They saw at least twenty motor boats with water pumps, sent by authorities. The row of water pipes looked like guns. The roaring of the machines and water made Sang Sang and Xi Ma excited for quite some time. People could hear the warning gongs signaling that an embankment had been breached somewhere, anytime, day or night.

Youmadi school naturally was a key organization to be protected. A dam was built surrounding it and some households. There was a bigger dam outside this dam.

邱二爷家在大坝里。

桑桑的母亲对邱二妈说："万一大坝出了事，你们就住到我家来。"面对着还在不断上涨的水，人心惶惶。

但孩子们总也紧张不起来。这个水世界，倒使他们感到有无穷的乐趣。他们或用洗澡的木盆，或干脆摘下门板来，坐在上面，当作小船划出去。他们没有看见过海，但想象中，海也就是这个样子：白茫茫，白茫茫，一望无边。不少人家的屋中已经进水，鲤鱼跳到锅台上的事情也已经听说。

桑桑和细马一人拿了一把鱼叉。他们来到水稍微浅一些的地方，寻找着从河里冲上来的鲤鱼。他们走着走着，随时都可能惊动一条大鱼，只见它箭一样射出去，留下一条长长的水痕。两个人欢快地在水中喊叫。

细马马上要走了。他没有想到在他将要离去时，竟能碰上如此让他激动的大水。他和桑桑一起，整天在水中玩耍，实在是开心极了。细马要抓住他在油麻地的最后时光，痛痛快快地玩。

邱二妈站在桑桑家门口，对桑桑的母亲叹息道："这两个小的，在一起玩一天是一天了。"

这天夜里，桑桑正在熟睡中，隐隐约约地听见到处有锣声和喊叫声。母亲点了灯过来，推着桑桑："醒醒，醒醒，好像出事了。"这里正说着，门被急促地敲响了："校长，师娘，开门哪！"

Old Qiu 2nd lived outside the big dam.

Sang Sang's mother told Madam Qiu 2nd, "Come to stay with us if something goes wrong with the big dam." Confronted with the ever-rising water, people were in a state of anxiety.

But children didn't get nervous. They found unlimited joy in the water world. They used wooden bathtubs and door planks as makeshift boats and floated in them. They hadn't seen the sea, but in their imagination, the sea was just like that -- a big expanse of water, unlimited. Water came into many households. It was heard that occasionally a carp would leap to the top of a stove.

Sang Sang and Xi Ma each took a fish spear. They came to a place where the water level was slightly lower, looking for carp washed up by the river. They walked and walked; they could startle big fish anytime. The fish would shoot up like an arrow, leaving behind it a long trace. Sang Sang and Xi Ma shouted joyfully in the water.

Xi Ma was to go soon. He didn't expect that he could see such an exciting flood before he left. He played happily in the water everyday with Sang Sang. Xi Ma wanted to play to his heart's content in these final days at Youmadi.

Madam Qiu 2nd stood at the door of the Sang's and sighed to Sang Sang's mother, "There are not that many days left for these two boys to play together."

One evening, when Sang Sang was asleep, he half-heard the sound of gongs and shouts from a distance. His mother lit up the lamp and pushed Sang Sang, "Wake up, wake up, something seems to have happened." At that moment, someone knocked hard on their door. "Principal, Madam Sang, open the door!"

门一打开，是邱二爷、邱二妈和细马湿淋淋地站在那里。

邱二爷说："大坝怕是决口了。"

邱二妈哭着："师娘，我们家完了。"

桑乔也起来了，问："进多深的水了？"

"快齐脖子了，还在涨呢。"邱二爷说。

母亲叫他们赶快进屋。

油灯下，所有的人都是一副恐惧的样子。桑桑的母亲总是问桑乔："这里面的一道坝撑得住吗？"桑乔说不好，就拿了手电走了出去。两个孩子也要跟着出去。桑乔说："去就去吧。"

三个人走了一会，就走到了坝上，往外一看，水快要越过坝来了。坝上有不少人，到处是闪闪烁烁的灯光。

这天夜里，邱二妈几乎没合眼，总在啼哭，说她的命真的很苦。

邱二爷一副木呆呆的样子，斜倚在桑桑家为他和邱二妈临时搭起的铺上。邱家的这份家产，经这场大水泡上几日，大概也就不值几文钱了。

与桑桑合睡一床的细马似乎心情也忽然沉重起来，不停地翻身，弄得桑桑一夜没有睡好。

第二天天才蒙蒙亮，邱二爷和邱二妈就爬上坝去看他们的房子。随即，邱二妈就瘫坐在堤上哭起来。

桑桑的母亲和桑桑的父亲都过来看，看到邱二爷的家已大半沉在水里了。

The door was opened; standing there were Old Qiu 2nd, Madam Qiu 2nd and Xi Ma standing there all soaked.

Old Qiu 2nd said, "There might be a breach in the big dam."

Madam Qiu 2nd cried, "Madam Sang, our home is finished."

Sang Qiao got up too. He asked, "How high is the water in your house?"

"Almost to the neck and still rising," said Old Qiu 2nd.

Sang Sang's mother hurriedly let them in.

Under the oil lamp, all looked scared. Sang Sang's mother kept asking Sang Qiao, "Can the inside dam inside stop the water?" Sang Qiao wasn't sure. He took his flashlight and went out. The two children wanted to follow him. Sang Qiao said, "OK then."

The three of them walked to the dam. They looked outside and saw water was about to cross over the dam. There were many people on the dam, and flashing lights everywhere.

Madam Qiu 2nd hardly closed her eyes all night. She cried and lamented their fate.

Old Qiu 2nd looked dumb, leaning on the bed the Sang's had quickly made up for him. After being soaked for a few days, the Qius' possessions would probably be worthless.

Xi Ma shared Sang Sang's bed. He seemed to have grown heavy-minded too, all of a sudden. He kept on turning, and Sang Sang wasn't able to sleep well.

The next day, at first glimmers of dawn, Old Qiu 2nd and Madam Qiu 2nd climbed on the dam to see their house. Madam Qiu 2nd sank on the dam and cried.

Sang Sang's parents came to look; the Qius' house stood more than half under water.

细马也爬到坝上。他蹲在那里，默默地看着水面上的屋脊、烟囱上立着的一只羽毛潮湿的水鸟。

那份在邱二妈眼里，细马以及细马的父亲就是冲着它来的家产，真的应了一句话：泡汤了。

4

大水差不多在一个月后，才完全退去。

田里的稻秧，已经全部淹死。到处烂乎乎的，几天好太阳一晒，空气里散发着一股腐烂的气息。

邱二爷家的房屋，地基已被水泡松，墙也被水泡酥，屋体已经倾斜，是非拆不可了。现在只能勉强住着。屋里的家具，十有八九已被泡坏。邱家几代传下的最值钱的一套红木家具，虽然在第二天就被邱二爷和细马、桑桑打捞上来，弄到油麻地小学的教室里，但因浸了水，榫松了，变形了。

这几天，桑桑就尽量与细马呆在一起。因为他知道，道路一通，细马马上就要离去了。

邱二爷不想再留细马多呆些日子了，对邱二妈说："给他收拾收拾吧。"

邱二妈说："早收拾好了。你早点送他回去吧。"

这天一大早，细马就来桑桑家告别了。

Xi Ma climbed to the dam too. He squatted there, silently gazing at the ridge of the Qius' house, and a water bird with wet feathers standing on the chimney above the surface of the water.

In Madam Qiu 2nd's eyes, Xi Ma and his father had been after their assets. But now, they were indeed gone.

4

The flood didn't retreat until almost one month later.

The rice seedlings in the fields had been drowned. It was rotten everywhere. The sun shone for a few days, and then there was the smell of decay in the air.

The earth foundation of Old Qiu 2nd's house had been soaked loose in the flood, so had the walls. The house was tilted, and there was no other way but to demolish it. It was just hanging there for the moment. Most of the furniture was badly damaged. There was a set of mahogany furniture that had been in the family for generations; although they took it out and moved it to the safety of a classroom of Youmadi school the next day, it was still soaked, loose and deformed.

Sang Sang tried to be with Xi Ma as much as possible these days. He knew Xi Ma would leave as soon as the road was clear.

Old Qiu 2nd didn't want to keep Xi Ma any more. He said to his wife, "Pack for Xi Ma."

She replied, "I packed for him long ago. You send him home."

Early one morning, Xi Ma came to the Sang's to say goodbye.

桑乔把手放在细马肩上很久："别忘了油麻地。"

桑桑的母亲说："有空回来看看二爷二妈。"

桑桑不知道说什么，就在那儿傻站着。

细马上路了。

大家都来送行。

邱二妈只把细马送到路上，就回去了。桑桑的母亲看到了，对细马说了一声"一路好好走"，就转过身去看邱二妈。邱二妈正在屋里哭，见了桑桑的母亲说："说走就走了……"泪珠就顺着她显然已经苍老了的脸往下滚。

细马走后，桑桑一整天都是一副落寞的样子。

邱二爷把细马送到县城，给细马买了一张长途汽车票，又买了一些路上吃的东西。邱二爷很想将细马一直送回家，但他有点羞于见到细马的父亲。再则，细马已经大了，用不着他一直送到底了。

离上车时间还早，两人坐在长途汽车站的候车室里，都默然无语。

细马上车后，将脸转过去看邱二爷。他看到邱二爷的眼睛潮湿着站在秋风里，一副疲惫而衰老的样子。细马还发现，邱二爷的背从未像今天这样驼，肩胛从未瘦得像今天这样隆起，脸色也从未像今天这样枯黑——枯黑得就像此刻在秋风中飘忽的梧桐老叶。

Sang Qiao put his hand on Xi Ma's shoulder for a long time, "Don't forget Youmadi."

Sang Sang's mother said, "Come back to see your uncle and aunt when you have time."

Sang Sang didn't know what to say; he just stood there, feeling foolish.

Xi Ma set out.

They all came to see him off.

After accompanying Xi Ma to the road, Madam Qiu 2nd went back home. Sang Sang's mother had told Xi Ma, "Take care of yourself on your way". She turned to look at Madam Qiu 2nd, who was sobbing in the room. She said to Sang Sang's mother, "He left just like that..." Tears rolled down her aging face.

Sang Sang felt lonely for the whole day.

Old Qiu 2nd went with Xi Ma to the town and bought a ticket for the long-distance bus, and food for the journey. He wanted to take Xi Ma home, but he was ashamed to see Xi Ma's father. Furthermore, Xi Ma was old enough to go on his own.

There was still quite some time before departure. The two of them sat in the waiting room of the long-distance bus station, silently.

Xi Ma got on the bus and turned to look at Old Qiu 2nd. The old man stood in the autumn wind, his eyes wet and looking tired and aged. Xi Ma had never seen him so hunched over, his shoulders never so thin -- they seemed to perch on his body. His face had never been so withered and dark -- like the floating parasol leaves in the autumn wind.

细马将脸转过去哭了。

车开动之后，细马又一次转过脸来。他看到了一双凄苦的目光……

傍晚，邱二爷回来了。这天晚上，他和邱二妈感到了一种无底的空虚和孤寂。老两口一夜未睡。清淡的月光，从窗外照进来，也把窗外的一株竹影投进来，直投在他们的脸上。秋风一吹，竹子一摇，那些影子就虚虚幻幻地晃动着。

一夜，他们几乎无语。只是邱二妈问了一句："孩子不知走到哪儿了。"邱二爷回答了一句："我也说不好呢。"

第二天黄昏时，桑桑正要帮着将邱二爷的几只在河坡上吃草的羊赶回邱二爷家时，偶然抬头一看，见路上正走过一个背着包袱的孩子来。他几乎惊讶得要跳起来：那不是细马吗？但他不相信，就揉了揉眼睛，仔细地看着：细马！就是细马！他扔掉手中赶羊的树枝，翻过大堤，一路往邱二爷家跑，一边跑，一边大叫："细马回来了！细马回来了……"

桑乔正站在校门口问："你说是谁回来了？"

桑桑脚步不停："细马！是细马回来了！"他一口气跑到邱二爷家，对邱二爷和邱二妈说："二爷，二妈，细马、细马……细马他……他回来了"

邱二爷和邱二妈站在那儿不动，像在梦里。

Xi Ma turned his face and cried.

When the bus started, Xi Ma turned his face once again. He saw a pair of tormented eyes...

At dusk, Old Qui 2nd came home. In the evening, he and his wife felt a bottomless emptiness and loneliness. They didn't sleep for the whole night. The clear and light moon shone from the window, projected the shadow of a bamboo outside the window on their face. When the autumn wind blew, the bamboo swayed, and the shadow vibrated, creating an unreal atmosphere.

They had almost nothing to say for the whole night. She asked once, "I wonder where he is now." Old Qiu 2nd replied, "I'm not sure either."

At dusk the next day, Sang Sang was to help Old Qiu 2nd drive home the goats eating grass on the river slope. He raised his head by chance and saw a boy walking over carrying a cloth-wrapped package. He was surprised and almost jumped up, wasn't that Xi Ma? Sang Sang couldn't believe it. He rubbed his eyes. He looked at the boy carefully, it was indeed Xi Ma! He threw away the branch in his hand, which he used to drive the goats. He climbed the big dam and ran to Old Qiu 2nd's house, shouting, "Xi Ma is back! Xi Ma is back..."

Sang Qiao stood at the entrance of the school. He asked, "Who did you say is back?"

Sang Sang didn't stop, "Xi Ma! It is Xi Ma back!" He ran to Old Qiu 2nd's house in one breath, and said to the couple, "Old Qiu 2nd, Madam Qiu 2nd, Xi Ma, Xi Ma... Xi Ma is back... He is back..."

The couple stood there motionless as if in a dream.

“细马回来啦！”桑桑用手指了一下黄昏中的路，然后迎着细马跑过去。

邱二爷和邱二妈急匆匆地跑到门口，朦朦胧胧地看到，大路上，真的有一个孩子背着包袱正往这边走过来。

等邱二爷和邱二妈跑到路口时，桑桑已背着包袱，和细马走到他们的跟前……

5

细马是在车开出去一个小时后下的车。

车在路上，细马眼前总是出现邱二爷的目光。油麻地的一切，也都在他心里不住地闪现。他终于叫了起来：“不好啦，我把东西落在车站啦！”驾驶员将车停下后，他就拿了包袱下了车，然后坐在路上，又拦了一辆回头的车，就又回到了县城。

当天晚上，一家人除了哭哭笑笑，就是邱二妈不时地说：“你回来干吗？你回来干吗？”就不知再说些其他什么。

第二天，邱二妈看着随时都可能坍塌的房子，对邱二爷说：“还是让他回去吧。”

细马听到了，拿了根树枝，将羊赶到田野去了。

几天后，邱二爷的房子就全推倒了。好好一幢房子，眨眼的工夫，就只剩下一堆废墟。眼见着天气一天凉似一天，就

"Xi Ma is back!" Sang Sang pointed to the road in dusk, and ran to Xi Ma.

The old couple hurried to the door, and they saw half clearly that there was indeed a boy walking over with a cloth-wrapped package, on the road.

When they ran to the junction of the road, Sang Sang was carrying Xi Ma's package and walked with Xi Ma towards them...

5

Xi Ma had gotten off the bus one hour after it set out.

Old Qiu 2nd's eyes had been flashing in front of his eyes all the time, so did everything at Youmadi. Finally he shouted, "Damn, I left my things at the station." The driver stopped the bus; Xi Ma took his package, got off the bus, stood on the road, stopped a returning bus and went back to the town.

In the evening, the Qiu family cried and laughed. Madam Qiu 2nd said constantly, "Why are you back? Why are you back?" But she didn't know what else to say.

The second day, Madam Qiu 2nd looked at the house which would collapse anytime and said to her husband,, "You'd better ask Xi Ma to go home."

Xi Ma heard it. He picked up a branch and drove the goats to the field.

A few days later, Old Qiu 2nd's house fell down. Such a great house -- now, in the blink of an eye, it was just a pile of remains. It got colder and colder day after day, and the family built a

临时搭了一个矮屋。一家人倒也并不觉得什么，日子过得平平常常、欢欢喜喜的。邱二妈仍是一尘不染的样子，在家烧饭、种菜，细马放羊，邱二爷有集市时就去集市上当他的掮客，没有集市时，就到田里做些农活。一有空，一家三口总要走过桥来，到桑桑家来玩。有时，细马晚上过来，与桑桑呆在一起，觉得还没有呆得过瘾，就站在河边喊："我不回去睡觉啦！"就睡在桑桑的床上。

一天，桑桑跑回来对母亲说："细马不再叫二爷二妈了，改叫爸爸妈妈了。"

细马晚上再过来，桑桑的母亲就问："听说细马不再叫二爷二妈了，改叫爸爸妈妈了。"

细马脸微微一红，走到一边，跟桑桑玩去了。

油麻地又多了一户平常而自足的人家。

但就在这年冬天，邱二爷病倒了。实际上邱二爷早在夏天时，就有了病兆：吃饭时，老被噎住，要不，吃下去的东西，不一会儿又吐出来。秋天将尽时，他就日见消瘦下来，很快发展到一连几天不能吃进去一碗粥。但邱二爷坚持着，有集市时仍去集市做掮客。他只想多多地挣钱。他必须给细马留下一幢像样一点的房子。入冬后的一天，他在集市上晕倒了，脸在砖上磕破了，流了不少血。是人把他扶回了家。第二天，邱二妈要找人将邱二爷护送到城里看病。邱二爷坚决

small, temporary house. They didn't greatly feel their loss, and returned to a normal and happy life. Madam Qiu 2nd was still spotless, cooking and growing vegetables at home. Xi Ma grazed the goats. Old Qiu 2nd still went to the market, returning to his profession as a broker. When the market was closed, he farmed. Whenever they had time, the three of them would cross the bridge and came to see the Sangs. Sometimes Xi Ma came in the evening to play with Sang Sang. He didn't want to go home and would shout at the riverside, "I am not going home to sleep." He would then share a bed with Sang Sang.

One day, Sang Sang ran to his mother and told her, "Xi Ma began to call Old Qui 2nd and Madam Qiu 2nd mum and dad."

Xi Ma came in the evening. Sang Sang's mother asked, "I heard that you call them 'mum' and 'dad' now."

Xi Ma's face turned slightly red. He walked to the side and played with Sang Sang.

There was now another ordinary and contented family at Youmadi.

However, Old Qui 2nd fell ill in the winter. In fact, symptoms had shown as early as in summer. He often choked while eating, or he would throw up what he had just eaten. When the autumn was near its end, he became thinner all the time. For several days, he couldn't finish a bowl of congee. But Old Qiu 2nd still struggled on. Whenever the market was active, he would go to do his broker's job. He just wanted to make some money. He had to leave Xi Ma with a decent house. One winter day in the market, he fainted. His face was torn on a brick and there was a lot of blood. People supported him, and led him home. The next day, Madam Qiu 2nd wanted to

地拒绝了："不要瞎花那个钱，我知道我得了什么病。"夜里，他对邱二妈说："我得了绝症。细马他爷爷就是得的这个病。是根本治不好的。"但邱二妈不听他的，到处求医问药。后来，听说一个人吃中药把这病吃好了，就把人家的方子要过来，去镇上抓了几十服中药。这时，已是腊月了。

这天早上，细马没有放羊，却拿了一把镐、一只竹篮离开了家门。

桑桑问："你去哪儿？要干什么？"

细马说："中药里头，得放柳树须子，我去河边刨柳树须子。"

桑桑的母亲正好走过来，说："桑桑，你去帮细马一起刨吧。"

这一年的冬天冷得有点异常。河里结了厚冰，让人无法汲水。因此，一早上，到处传来用榔头敲冰砸洞的声音。整个世界，都冻得硬邦邦的，仿佛天上的太阳都被冻住了。风倒不大，但空气里注满了寒气。

细马和桑桑在河边找到了一棵柳树。

细马挥镐砸下去，那冻土居然未被敲开，只是留下一道白痕。细马往手上啐了一口唾沫，咬着牙，用了更大的劲，又将镐砸了下去。这一回，镐尖被卡在冻土里。细马将镐晃动了半天，才将它拔出来。

get somebody to escort him to the city to see a doctor. But Old Qiu 2nd refused point-blank. "Don't waste money. I know what's wrong with me." In the evening, he told his wife, "My illness is terminal. Xi Ma's grandpa had it too. It can't be cured." Madam Qiu 2nd wouldn't listen to him. She went to see doctors and searched for drugs everywhere. Later, she heard that someone had taken Chinese herbs and was cured; she asked for the prescription and went to the town to get dozens of medical herbs. It was already the twelfth moon.

One morning, Xi Ma didn't go to graze the goats. He carried a pickaxe and a basket and left home.

Sang Sang asked, "Where are you going? What are you doing?"

Xi Ma said, "There have to be willow tassels in Chinese herbs. I am going to the riverside to dig some willow tassels."

Sang Sang's mother happened to come over. She said, "Sang Sang, go help Xi Ma dig some willow tassels."

It was an extraordinarily cold winter. There was thick ice on the river and people couldn't easily get water. The sound of people chopping the ice and drilling holes was heard everywhere in the morning. The whole world was frozen hard; the sun seemed to be frozen too. The wind wasn't too strong, yet cold filled in the air.

Xi Ma and Sang Sang found a willow tree near the river.

Xi Ma lifted his pickaxe and struck down, but the frozen earth wasn't broken; only a line of white appeared. Xi Ma spit on his hands, clenched his teeth, and struck the earth harder. This time, the point of his pickaxe stuck in the frozen earth. Xi Ma shook the pickaxe for quite some time before taking it out.

不一会儿，桑桑就看到，细马本来就有裂口的手，因连续受到剧烈震动，流出血来。血将镐柄染红了。桑桑就把竹篮子扔在地上，从细马手中夺过镐来，替换下细马。但桑桑没有细马力气大，进展很慢。细马说："还是我来吧。"就又抢过了镐。

这柳树的根仿佛就没有须子，刨了那么大一个坑，树根都露出一大截来了，还未见到须子。桑桑很疑惑：能弄到柳树须子吗？但细马不疑惑，只管一个劲地去刨。头上出了汗，他把帽子扔在地上，头在冷空气里，飘散着雾状的热气。他又把棉袄也脱下了。

总算见到了柳树须子。一撮一撮的，像老头的胡子。

桑桑说："这一棵柳树的须子，就够了。"

细马说："不够。"因为细马在挑这些柳树须子时很苛刻。他只要白嫩白嫩的，像一条条细白的虫子一样的须子。黑的，或红的，一概不要。一棵柳树，他也就选一二十根。

细马穿好棉袄，戴上帽子，扛了镐，又去找第二棵柳树。

桑桑几次说："够了，够了。"

但细马总是说："不够，不够。"

桑桑很无奈，只好在寒风里陪伴着细马。

到了中午，竹篮子里，已有大半筐柳树须子。那须子在这冰天雪地，生命都似乎被冻结了的冬季，实在是好看。那

After a while, Sang Sang saw blood come out of Xi Ma's hands, which already had cracks, and now cracked further after heavy digging. The blood dyed the pickaxe handle red. Sang Sang threw the basket to the ground, and grabbed the pickaxe from Xi Ma. He replaced Xi Ma in digging, but he wasn't as strong and the progress was slow. Xi Ma said, "Let me do it." He grabbed the pickaxe again.

It seemed that there were no tassels on the root of this willow tree. They had dug such a big hole and such a big chunk of the root had exposed, but they still didn't see the tassels. Sang Sang was very puzzled. Could they really get tassels? But Xi Ma wasn't in doubt. He just tried hard to dig. There was sweat on his forehead. He threw his hat to the ground. In the cold air, his head emitted misty hot air. He took off his cotton-padded jacket too.

Finally they saw some willow tassels -- they were like the beard of an old man, tuff by tuff.

Sang Sang said, "The tassels of this willow tree are enough."

Xi Ma said, "No." He was fastidious in picking tassels. He wanted the white and tender ones, like those white and slim worms. He didn't want the black or red ones. He had picked only ten or twenty from the tree.

Xi Ma put on his cotton-padded jacket and hat. He picked up his pickaxe and went to find the second willow tree.

Sang Sang said several times, "It's enough, enough."

But Xi Ma always said, "No, no."

Sang Sang couldn't persuade him. He just followed Xi Ma in the cold wind.

By noon, there were more than half a basket of willow tassels, looking beautiful in the winter of ice and snow, when

么白，那么嫩，一根一根，仿佛都是活的，仿佛你一不留神，它们就会从竹篮里爬出去。太阳一照，就仿佛盛了半竹篮细细的银丝。

邱二妈看见这大半竹篮柳树须子时，眼睛红了。

可是，邱二爷未能等到春季来临，就去世了。临去时，他望着细马，眼睛里只有歉疚与深深的遗憾，因为他终于没有能够给细马留下一幢好房子。

送走邱二爷以后，邱二妈倒也不哭，仿佛悲伤已尽，已没有什么了。她只是一天到晚地沉默着，做她该做的事情：给细马烧饭，给细马洗衣服，夜里起来给细马盖被细马蹬翻了的被子，晚上端上一木盆热水让细马将脚放进去，然后她蹲下去给他好好搓洗……

邱二妈在神情恍惚了十几天之后，这天一早，就来到桑桑家，站在门口问桑桑的母亲："师娘，你看见二爷了吗？"

桑桑的母亲赶紧拉住邱二妈的手，道："二妈，你先进来坐一会儿。"

"不了，我要找二爷呢。这个人不知道哪儿去了。"邱二妈又见到了桑桑，"桑桑，看见你二爷了吗？"

桑桑有点害怕了，瞪着眼睛，摇着头。

"我要去找他，我要去找他……"邱二妈说着，就走了。

life itself seemed to have frozen. The tassels were so white and tender, one by one. They seemed to be alive, as if they would climb out of the bamboo basket if one were not careful for a moment. When the sun shone on them, they looked like thin silver.

Seeing the more than half a basket of willow tassels, Madam Qiu 2nd's eyes turned red.

Still, Old Qiu 2nd passed away before spring. Before he died, he looked at Xi Ma, full of apologies and deep regret in his eyes. He hadn't managed to leave a great house to Xi Ma.

Madam Qiu 2nd didn't cry after Old Qiu 2nd died. It seemed the sadness had all gone and there was nothing left. She was silent all day long, doing her work -- cooking and washing for Xi Ma, getting up in the evening to cover Xi Ma with a quilt, which had been kicked off by the boy in the night; getting a wooden pan of hot water and putting Xi Ma's feet in it, squatting down to wash his feet...

After she had been in a trance for more than a dozen days, Madam Qiu 2nd came to the Sang's early one morning. She stood at the door and asked Sang Sang's mother, "Madam Sang, have you seen Old Qiu 2nd?"

Sang Sang's mother hurried to take her hand, "Madam Qiu 2nd, come in and sit down."

"No, I need to find Old Qiu 2nd. Where has he gone?" She saw Sang Sang, "Sang Sang, have you seen Old Qiu 2nd?"

Sang Sang was a little bit scared. He stared at her and shook his head.

"I'm going to look for him, I'm going to look for him..." She left.

桑桑的母亲就一直看着邱二妈的背影，直到她消失在一幢草房子的拐角处。她进屋来对桑乔说："这可怎么办？邱二妈的脑子出毛病了。"

桑乔似乎并不特别吃惊："听人说，她母亲差不多也是在这个年纪上，脑子出了毛病。"

在细马未来之前，邱二妈和邱二爷一直相依为命，做了几十年的好夫妻。桑桑的母亲总记得，邱二爷去集市做掮客时，邱二妈就会在差不多的时候，站到路口上去等邱二爷回来。而邱二爷回来时，不是给她带回她喜爱吃的东西，就是带回她喜欢用的东西。相比之下，邱二爷显得比邱二妈老得多。但邱二爷喜欢邱二妈比他年少。邱二爷喜欢邱二妈总去梳她的头，整理她的衣服。喜欢与打扮得很俏的邱二妈一起去桑桑家串门，一起搬张凳子到打麦场上看电影或者看小戏……邱二爷离不开邱二妈，而邱二妈可能更离不开邱二爷。现在邱二爷居然撇下她走了。

邱二妈必须要找到邱二爷。她一路问下去："见到我家二爷了吗？"

这天，细马放羊回来，见邱二妈不在家，就找到桑桑家，见了桑桑，问："我妈在你家吗？"

桑桑摇了摇头："不在我家。"

细马就一路呼唤下去。当时，天已黑了，每户人家都已点了灯，正在吃晚饭。乡村的夜晚，分外寂静。人们都听到了细马的呼唤声。

Sang Sang's mother looked at her back until she disappeared at the corner of a straw house. She came into the room and said to Sang Qiao, "What's to be done? Madam Qiu 2nd seems to have gone mad."

Sang Qiao didn't seem to be too surprised, "I heard her mother was just like that at her age."

Before Xi Ma came, Madam Qiu 2nd and Old Qiu 2nd had only each other to rely upon. They were a close couple for decades. Sang Sang's mother always remembered that when he went to the market to work, Madam Qiu 2nd would always wait for him at the junction when it was time to come home. He always brought back her favorite food or other things. Old Qiu 2nd looked much older than his wife, but was happy that Madam Qiu 2nd was younger than he was. He liked to watch her comb her hair and tidy her clothes. He liked to visit the Sangs with his prettily-dressed wife. He liked to carry a stool and go with her to the wheat threshing ground to watch a film or a small show... Old Qiu 2nd couldn't do with his wife. His wife similarly depended on him. Now he had passed away, leaving her on her own.

Madam Qiu 2nd just had to find her husband. She asked people along the road, "Have you seen Old Qiu 2nd?"

Xi Ma came home from grazing his goats and didn't see Madam Qiu 2nd. He went to the Sang's house to look for her. He saw Sang Sang and asked, "Is my mum here?"

Sang Sang shook his head, "No, not here."

Xi Ma called for her along the road. It was already dark. Each household had lit its lamp and was having supper. It was extremely silent in the evening in the village. Everyone heard Xi Ma calling.

桑桑和母亲就循着细马的叫声，找到了细马，让他回家："你妈她自己会回来的。"硬把他劝了回来。然后，由桑桑和妹妹给细马端来了晚饭。细马不肯吃，让饭菜一直放在饭桌上。

桑桑和母亲走后，细马就一直坐在路边，望着月光下那条路。

第二天一早，细马来到桑桑家，将门上的钥匙给了桑桑的母亲："师娘，你帮着看一下家，我去找我妈。"

桑桑的父母亲都不同意。但细马说："我找找就回家，我不走远。"临走时，又对桑桑说："桑桑，你帮我看一下羊。"就走了。

细马一走就是七天。

桑桑天天一早上就将羊赶到草坡上去，像细马一样，将那群羊好好照应着。但这天晚上，他把羊赶回羊圈，看到细马家依然锁着门之后，回到家哭了："细马怎么还不回来？"

又过了两天，这天傍晚，桑桑正要将羊从草坡上赶回家，看到西边霞光里，走来了细马和邱二妈。

听到桑桑的叫声，无数的人都走到路口上来看。

邱二妈是被细马搀着走回来的。

所有的人，都只是静静地望着他们，没有一个人说话。

细马满身尘埃。脚上的鞋已被踏坏，露着脚趾头。眼睛因为瘦弱而显得更眍，几颗大门牙，显得更大。令人惊奇的

Sang Sang and his mother traced Xi Ma's calling and found Xi Ma, and asked him to go home, "Your mum will come back herself." They persuaded him to come back. Sang Sang and his younger sister brought dinner to Xi Ma. But he wouldn't eat; he left his food on the table.

When Sang Sang and his mother left, Xi Ma sat on the side of the road, looking at the road under the moon for a long time.

Early next morning, Xi Ma came to the Sang's. He handed the key to his house to Sang Sang's mother, "Madam Sang, please look after my house. I'm going to look for my mum."

Sang Sang's parents didn't want to let him go. But Xi Ma said, "I'll be back soon. I won't go too far." Before he left, he said to Sang Sang, "Sang Sang, take care of my goats for me." He left.

Xi Ma was gone for seven days.

Early every morning, Sang Sang drove the goats to the grass slope, looked after the goats well, just as had Xi Ma. One evening, he drove the goats back to the pen and saw Xi Ma's door still locked. He went home and cried, "Why is Xi Ma still not back?"

Two days later, at dusk, Sang Sang was about to drive the goats back home from the grass slope when he saw Xi Ma and Madam Qiu 2nd in the western rays.

Sang Sang shouted, and many people came to the junction of the road to have a look.

Madam Qiu 2nd walked back, supported by Xi Ma.

Everyone looked at them in silence.

Xi Ma was covered with dust all over. His shoes were partly already worn off, his toes exposed. His eyes looked more

是，邱二妈仍然是一副干干净净的样子，头发竟一丝不乱。人们看到，那枚簪子上的绿玉，在霞光里变成了一星闪闪发亮的、让人觉得温暖的橘红色。

6

细马卖掉了所有的羊，在桑桑一家的帮助下，将邱二妈送进县城医院。大约过了两个月，邱二妈的病居然治好了。

这天，细马来找桑乔："桑校长，你们学校还缺不缺课桌？"

桑乔说："缺。"

细马说："想买树吗？"

"你要卖树？"

"我要卖树。"

"多少钱一棵？"

"那要论大小。"

桑乔笑起来。他觉得眼前这个细马，口吻完全是一个大人，但样子又是一个小孩。

"你们想买，就去看看。都是笔直的楝树。一共十六棵。"

"你卖树干什么？"

"我有用处。"

"你跟你妈商量了吗？"

"不用跟她商量。"细马一副当家做主的样子。

sunken because he had gotten thinner, his front teeth bigger. Surprisingly enough, Madam Qiu 2nd still looked clean, without one hair in disorder. People saw that the green jade on her hairpin glimmered in the rays and radiated warm orange.

6

Xi Ma sold all the goats. With the help of the Sangs, he sent Madam Qiu 2nd to the hospital in town. About two mouths later, she was cured.

Xi Ma went to see Sang Qiao one day, "Principal Sang, do you need desks at school?"

Sang Qiao said, "Yes."

Xi Ma: "Do you want to buy trees?"

"You have trees to sell?"

"Yes."

"How much for one tree?"

"It depends on the size."

Sang Qiao laughed. He felt Xi Ma was talking like an adult, but still looked like a child.

"Come have a look. I have some straight chinaberries, sixteen in total."

"Why do you want to sell your trees?"

"I have my reasons."

"Have you talked with your mum?"

"There is no need." Xi Ma looked as if he were now the decision-maker in the family.

“好的。过一会儿，我过去看看。”

“那我就卖给你，不卖给别人了。”

桑乔看着细马走过桥去，然后很有感慨地对桑桑的母亲说：“这孩子大了。”

桑桑的母亲就用脚轻轻踢了一下正在玩耍的桑桑：“我们家桑桑，还只知道玩鸽子呢。”

细马在桑乔这里讨了一个好价钱，卖了十二棵树。还有四棵，他没有卖，说以后盖房子，要做大梁。

细马拿了卖树的钱，天天一早就坐到大河边上去。

大河里，总有一些卖山羊的船行过。那些雪白的山羊装在船舱里，不停地拥挤、跃动，从眼前经过时，就觉得翻着一船的浪花。

细马要买羊，要买一群羊。

但细马并不着急买。他要仔细打听价钱，仔细观察那些羊。他一定要用最低的价钱买最上等的羊。他很有耐心。这份耐心绝对是大人才有的。有几回，生意眼看就要做成了，但细马又放弃了。船主就苦笑：“这个小老板，太精。”

细马居然用了十天的工夫，才将羊买下。一共五十只。只只白如秋云，绒如棉絮。船主绝对是做了出血的买卖，但他愿意。因为，他一辈子还没有见过如此精明能干的孩子。

大平原上，就有了一个真正的牧羊少年。

"OK, I'll come to have a look later on."

"I'll sell them to you, not others."

Sang Qiao saw Xi Ma walk across the bridge. He said to Sang Sang's mother with emotion, "The child has grown up."

Sang Sang's mother kicked Sang Sang lightly, who was playing on the side, "Our Sang Sang knows only about playing with pigeons."

Xi Ma got a good price from Sang Qiao and sold twelve trees. He kept four, saying they would be used as big beams when he built a house in the future.

Xi Ma took the money and sat on the riverside early in the morning.

There were always boats passing by on the big river, selling goats. The snow-white goats were kept in the cabin, crowding each other and constantly jumping about. When a boat passed by, it looked like a boatful of waves.

Xi Ma wanted to buy a flock of goats.

But he was not in a hurry. He wanted to inquire about the price, and observed the goats carefully. He had to buy the best goats at the lowest price. He was patient -- the kind of patience only a grown-up had. A few times, he almost got a deal, but he still refused. The owner of the boat would smile bitterly, "This little boss is too cunning."

It took Xi Ma ten days to buy the goats. He bought fifty, each as white as clouds in autumn, and as soft as cotton wadding. The owner of the boat absolutely took a loss, but he was willing. He had never seen such a clever and capable child in his life.

There was a true shepherd on the big plain from then on.

桑桑读六年级时，细马的羊群就已经发展到一百多只了。这年秋天，他卖掉了七十多只羊，只留了五只强壮的公羊和二十五只特别能下崽的母羊。然后，他把卖羊的钱统统买了刚出窑的新砖。他发誓，他一定要给妈妈造一幢大房子。

桑桑记得，那堆砖头运回来时，是秋后的一个傍晚。

砖头码在一块平地上。一色的红砖，高高地码起来，像一堵高大的城墙。

邱二妈不停地用手去抚摸这些砖头，仿佛那是一块块金砖。

“我要爬到顶上去看看。”细马搬来一架梯子，往上爬去。

桑桑看见了细马，仰头问：“细马，你爬上去干什么？”

细马站在砖堆顶上：“我看看！”

桑桑一家人，就都走出门来看。

夕阳正将余辉反射到天上，把站在砖堆顶上的细马映成了一个细长条儿。余辉与红砖的颜色融在一起，将细马染成浓浓的土红色……

When Sang Sang was in grade six, Xi Ma's flock had grown to more than one hundred. He sold more than seventy that autumn. He only kept five strong males and twenty-five females which were extremely good at breeding. He bought new bricks just out of the kiln with all the money. He promised he would build a big house for his mum.

Sang Sang remembered, it was at dusk at the end of autumn when the pile of bricks were shipped.

The bricks were placed on a flat surface, all red and piled high, like a tall wall.

Madam Qiu 2nd kept touching the bricks all the time, as if they were gold.

"I am going to climb up to have a look." Xi Ma took a ladder and climbed up.

Sang Sang saw Xi Ma, raised his head and asked, "Xi Ma, what are you doing."

Xi Ma stood on the top of the pile, "Just having a look!"

The Sangs all came out to have a look.

The setting sun projected its remaining rays to the sky, casting Xi Ma on the top of the brick pile as a long, slim figure. The remaining rays and the redness of the bricks merged, dyed Xi Ma into a thick earthy red...

This book is edited and designed by the Editorial Committee of *Cultural China* series

Managing Editors: Xu Naiqing, Wang Youbu, Wu Ying
Project Editor: Wu Ying
Editor: Yang Xinci

Chinese Story by Cao Wenxuan
Translation by Sylvia Yu and Julian Chen

Interior and Cover Design: Yuan Yinchang, Xue Wenqing

ISBN-13: 978-1-60220-908-4
ISBN-10: 1-60220-908-1

Address any comments about *Straw Houses* to:

Better Link Press
99 Park Ave
New York, NY 10016
USA
or
Shanghai Press and Publishing Development Company
F 7 Donghu Road, Shanghai, China (200031)
Email: comments_betterlinkpress@hotmail.com

Computer typeset by Yuan Yinchang Design Studio, Shanghai
Printed in China by Shanghai Donnelley Printing Co. Ltd.

1 2 3 4 5 6 7 8 9 10